# PRAISE FOR *HOUSE ARREST:*

"This gripping novel in verse . . . is serious and funny, thrilling and touching, sweet and snarky. . . . Plenty of appeal for reluctant and enthusiastic readers alike." —*School Library Journal*

"Readers . . . will appreciate Holt's lessons of compassion and family above all." —*Booklist*

"Easy to read and strong on sibling devotion."—*Kirkus Reviews*

"Touches of humor lighten the mood, and Holt's firsthand knowledge of the subject . . . adds depth to this poignant drama without overwhelming it." —*Publishers Weekly*

"Moving. . . . Readers will nod their heads in sympathy with this guy who breaks the rules for all of the right reasons."
—*The Bulletin of the Center for Children's Books*

"Readers will want to stay with Timothy every step of the way. The characters are well-drawn and believable. . . . Timothy is a powerful and sympathetic voice." —*School Library Connection*

A Bank Street College of Education Best Book of the Year

# HOUSE ARREST

## K.A. HOLT

chronicle books · san francisco

First Chronicle Books LLC paperback edition, published in 2016.
Originally published in hardcover in 2015 by Chronicle Books LLC.

ISBN 978-1-4521-5648-4

The Library of Congress has cataloged the original edition as follows:
Holt, K. A., author.
 House arrest / by K.A. Holt.
   pages cm
 Summary: Young Timothy is sentenced to house arrest after impulsively
stealing a wallet, and he is forced to keep a journal into which he pours all
his thoughts, fears, and frustrations.
ISBN 978-1-4521-3477-2
 1. Diaries—Juvenile fiction. 2. Juvenile delinquents—Juvenile fiction.
3. Detention of persons—Juvenile fiction. [1. Novels in verse. 2. Diaries—
Fiction. 3. Juvenile delinquency—Fiction. 4. Detention of persons—
Fiction.] I. Title.

 PZ7.5.H65Ho 2015
 813.6—dc23


                     2014022151


Manufactured in China.

Design by Jennifer Tolo Pierce.
Typeset in Bodoni Six ITC and Vine Street.

10 9 8 7 6 5 4 3 2 1

Chronicle Books LLC
680 Second Street
San Francisco, CA 94107


Chronicle Books—we see things differently. Become part of our
community at www.chroniclekids.com.

*To my sweet Ike-a-saurus*

卌 卌 卌 卌 卌

卌 卌 卌 卌 卌

IIII IIII IIII IIII IIII
IIII IIII IIII I

WINTER

# WEEK 1

Boys don't write in journals,
unless it's court-ordered.
At least, this is what I've figured.

✹

I
I have
I have nothing
to say

✹

I am not allowed to have nothing to say.
Except on Tuesdays
when I go see Mrs. Bainbridge
who calls me Tim instead of Timothy.
I sit on her squishy couch
my mouth sealed shut
my eyes burning holes
in the leaves of all her plants.
She says I can call her Maureen.
But who would want to be called Maureen?

✳

Adjudicated delinquent.
I had to look up how to spell that.
Three times.
I don't feel like a delinquent
and I don't know what *adjudicated* means
(even after looking it up).
Sounds like a kung fu move.
I adjudicated you in your face!
HI-YA

✳

A whole year of this journal?
Maybe I will write about the other people I see.
Like José . . . just being José.
I will pretend his life is mine,
like I can still go hang out in our street
whenever I want.
Magnolia Circle. Where I've always lived.
With the manhole cover
that makes a perfect third base.

# WEEK 2

How do you let yourself
become a probation officer?
Is there a school for that?
A diploma?
Congrats, James, you have graduated
and are now
a complete
tool.

✺

James recommends
not writing any more things
like that last thing.
Otherwise
the judge will get mad.
Who knew my probation officer
could read my journal?
I would like it on record that that isn't fair.
Do you hear me, James?
Do you hear me, Mrs. Bainbridge?
Do you hear me, Judge?
A personal journal is very crowded
with so many eyes.

✹

James on Monday.
Mrs. Bainbridge on Tuesday.
School every day.
Home every day.
Nowhere else unless Mom is with me.
That's the schedule, Journal.
Got it?
It's pretty simple.
Like a court-ordered cage,
with a Mom-shaped lock.

✹

*You better take this journal seriously*,
James told me Monday.
*Or they'll throw you in juvie*
*so fast*
*your head will spin.*
As if my head isn't already spinning.

✹

On that day, weeks ago, I'd lost my head.
Everything foggy and frosty,
everything a dwarf name

from a fairy tale
that doesn't exist.
I remember I was so tired.
So
so
so
tired.
Levi had been sick the night before.
One of those nights with no nurse at home to help.
Mom had her hands full.
And I did, too.
Levi was bad sick.
So I helped.
Running for towels,
for meds,
for the heavy oxygen tanks,
for the suction machine,
for the spare trach tubes,
for the ties to keep the tube in his neck
so he could breathe
which he wasn't doing very well
that night
before the morning
when my head was full of fairy-tale dwarves
named Foggy and Frosty and Sleepy and Crazy.

❋

I will never know what I was thinking when I stole
that wallet,
because I wasn't thinking.
I wish everyone would stop asking.
There is no *what*
when there is no thinking.
There is just *is*-ing.
Things happen.
Things happened.
Just like that.
Snap.
It is what it is.
It was what it was.
So stop asking.
I was trying to help,
that's all.
But it was the opposite of help,
and I know that now.
I'm not sorry, though.
If you're wondering.
I'm just sorry I got caught.
Because it *would* have helped.
It would have.

# WEEK 3

James says I should take that last part out.
*You better be sorry*, he says
when he throws this journal into my chest
looking mad and disappointed.
A look they must give tests on
at Probation Officer University.
*This is not a joke, Timothy.*
*They'll throw you in juvie so fast*
*your head will spin.*
I mouth the words when he says them.
He doesn't like that.
But he needs new words.
He won't like it that I wrote that, either.
Oh, well.
Hey, James?
Suck it.

＊

When Levi was born my dad was still here.
Nine months ago.
Feels like nine years.
Dad's heart was beating in the same room as mine.

His lungs filled with the same air as mine.
His stomach filled with the same pizza as mine.
We had pepperoni that night
when Levi was born.
We high-fived our root beers.
Dad told the waitress,
*I have two boys now. How about that?*
And she gave us ice cream
for free.
And it was the best night.
Until it wasn't anymore.
Then the phone rang in the pitch-dark night
and José's mom answered because I was at their house.
Dad was at the hospital with Mom and Levi.
José's mom came to wake me up
but I was already awake.
And she drove me to the hospital
and she told me Levi was sick
and the doctors didn't know what it was
and it was bad
real bad
and they wanted me there
in case he died
so I could say good-bye

and none of it made sense
because Levi was a brand-new baby
and nothing happens to brand-new babies
because they are new and haven't hurt anyone yet.
And Dad still had pizza in his stomach
and so did I
from earlier that night
when everything was OK.
P.S. Levi did not die.
Not any time they told us he would.
And there were a lot of times.

❋

James.
Mrs. B.
I know you're reading, so listen up.
I'm thinking you guys don't know anything
about anything.
No offense.
But if you're going to understand what I'm
talking about
in this dumb journal
I'm going to need to explain some things
to your dumb faces.

No offense.
There are just so many things you have to understand
before you can really understand.
Understand?
So I can tell you about that day
that stealing day
but you're never going to know
what was going on in my head
because I don't know what was going on in my head
all I do know is what was going on in my life.

✳

Lesson One: trach.
You say it like *trake*
in case you didn't know.
It's a plastic tube
in Levi's neck.
Well, in a hole in Levi's neck,
a hole the doctor put there
so Levi can breathe.
The tube protects the hole
but it lets in a lot of germs
like a superhighway to his lungs,
so that's no good.

But breathing is good.
Kind of a lame trade-off, if you ask me.
I guess the trach is like a plastic nostril
in Levi's neck.
It has all the gross stuff that nostrils have:
slippery boogers
and slime
and gunk
and when he sneezes, these snot bullets shoot out.
So, yeah. It's a plastic nostril in your neck.
But it doesn't look like a nostril. Just a tube.
It saved Levi's life
and changed everyone else's.

✸

Sometimes I wonder what it's like
to breathe through your neck
instead of your face.
How does food taste
if you can't smell it?
Do your sinuses still hurt
when you're sick?
Does it tickle when you cough
out of the tube?
Does it feel weird when you swallow?

It must.
Because Levi chokes a lot.
When he chokes we use the suction machine
and it is so loud
like a jackhammer drinking a Slurpee.
It sucks all of the gunk out of the tube in his neck
so Levi can breathe easy again.
He always looks so relieved.
I wonder how that feels?

✳

José came over today.
He called me a felon
and laughed his head off.
He wanted me to come with him.
Cam's paintball party.
My answer:
*What part of house arrest don't you understand,*
*dummy?*
I told him I was getting a tracking device on my ankle
and if I leave the house
it will blow my whole leg off.
Even messier than paintball.
He believed me
so I laughed *my* head off.

# WEEK 4

James says I need to talk more about that day.
*Your journal*, he says,
in that eye-rolly way they must teach at
Probation Officer University,
*is to prove you are reflecting on what you did,*
*to prove house arrest is working,*
*to prove you don't need juvie to set you straight.*
*It is court-ordered, Timothy.*
*You know what that means, right?*
And that's when I shout,
*I'm* doing *it, right?*
*I'm* writing *in it, OK?*
He nods and looks kind of bored.
And I wonder, again, how this ever happened.

✸

There are a lot of things I know
that I shouldn't know
about why things are the way they are.
About Dad driving away and never coming back.
About his job he never went back to.
About Mom working nights for extra money.

14

About food coming from the church on the corner.
About Levi's medicine costing as much
as a pet space shuttle.
I know.
But I don't say I know.
But Mom knows I know.
Because she knows everything.
Except whether or not Dad is ever coming back.
No one knows that.
Well, maybe Dad does.

✻

A year is a long time
to write in a journal.
and never go to paintball parties.
That is not a haiku.

✻

José came over.
It was a quick visit.
His mom made a casserole for him to bring
which he thought was embarrassing.
So did I.
*Oh, we don't need a casserole!*

Mom said it in her fake-smile voice.
But I put it in the fridge for later.
It smelled so good.
Way better smelling than José
who punched me in the shoulder
and called me "smooth criminal"
even though I'm not smooth at all.
At all.

✳

That day.
Always in my head.
Won't go away.
Always in the mirror.
Written on my face.
That day.
When the guy's wallet was next to the credit card
swiper thing
at the checkout
and the manager and the guy looked out the window
at the car crash outside of the grocery store.
My breath came fast.

My vision did this weird pinpoint thing.

My brain went white.

So I leaned over, grabbed the wallet, kept walking.

The sun was bright.

The day was cold.

The wallet was heavier than I thought it would be.

I paid

one thousand

four hundred

forty-

five

dollars

and

thirty-

two

cents

on one shiny blue card.

Levi's medicine for one month.

I made it one and a half days before they caught me.

One and a half days of feeling like I could breathe.

One and a half days of trying to figure out how to tell Mom.

Then the police came.

They took me away.
But even worse?
They took the medicine away, too.
Man. I was really stupid then.

✳

White hair on his head
coming out his ears
creeping from his nose
BOBBY
his red name tag shouts it
as if your eyes are deaf.
When BOBBY took that credit card
he knew it wasn't right
the white hair in his nose
sucked in and out
like seaweed in the tide.
*My uncle's card.*
The sweat rolled down my face
getting in my eyes.
*Quite the generous uncle.*
That's what BOBBY said
when he swiped the card

handed over the medicine
never taking his eyes off me
even when the pharmacy door ding-dinged
and I turned around
looking back through the glass.
BOBBY watched me go,
his mouth a tight line
his hand in his white hair
searching for answers.

# WEEK 5

James frowned.

His little pig eyes narrowed.

*Better, but not great*, he said.

*Show more feelings*, he said.

*Prove you're not a sociopath*, he said.

*You prove* you're *not a sociopath*, I said,

slamming the journal shut

almost as hard as my heart slammed into my ribs.

*YOU prove it.*

You don't have to call me names, James.

Is making me feel worse part of your job?

Part of what they teach at

Probation Officer University?

I don't even know what sociopath means

but I know I'm not one.

I'm just a kid.

I'm just a kid.

✻

There are all these words I say every day.
Words I never even thought about before.
*Trach* is one.
You remember that one, right?
It rhymes with *brake* and *take.*
There is also *wedge*
which can mean something you shove under a door
to keep it open,
but in this case means a thing that Levi hangs on,
actually hangs,
with his butt in a sling made of blue jean material,
a sling that has lots of superstrong Velcro.
He hangs on the *wedge* so his *trach* stays *unobstructed.*
That sentence is my world now.
Levi's world.
Mom's world.
It doesn't seem normal, but it is an everyday
sentence now.
So I guess that makes it normal?
*Normal* is a word I never thought about before, either.
But now I think about it
a lot.

❋

I haven't done my homework in so long
I can't even remember.
I know this journal is not for confessing
homework sins,
but there you have it.
Levi is too sick.
Even with his nurse, Marisol,
and even with Mom
there aren't enough hands.
Marisol has to go home at night.
And Mom has to work.
And my hands have to help.
Instead of doing fractions.
Some things are more important than fractions.

❋

Hypothetically speaking,
what would happen if José does my math homework?
If I fail math will the judge get mad?
Could I go to juvie?
You know what should be on my math homework?
Q: What is 3 + 1?
A: The number of hours Timothy slept last night.

✸

I met José when we were in second grade.
His family moved in three houses down.
José has four sisters.
They are all crazy.
I think he likes to come to my house because it's quiet.
Even with Levi's jackhammer suction machine
and breathing alarms,
and snot bullets,
my house is still quieter
than a house filled with four sisters.
Believe it.

✸

You know,
the problem with babies is that you can't hate them.
You can try.
I tried.
But they have these fuzzy soft heads,
they have slurpy smiles.
Even when you stick out your tongue
or make a mean face
or give them a poke with your finger
they still have slurpy smiles.

It's really hard to hate a baby.
Even if you think about all the times before the baby
when your dad was at home and happy
and your mom never cried herself to sleep
at the kitchen table
even when you think about these times
you still can't hate a baby.
Stupid cute babies.
Complicating everything.

# WEEK 6

Mrs. Bainbridge called that last part of the journal
a breakthrough.
I don't know about that.
Maybe she said that because I never talk in her office
so she was excited to see so many *feeling* words
all on one page.
I don't feel like I've broken through anything, though.
Really.
Maybe some things have broken through me?

❋

The thing is,
and I don't know if I should say this,
but house arrest isn't *so* bad.
Pretty much,
I've been on "house arrest" since Levi came home.
That's not bad.
Just how it is.
It's not really safe to take him anywhere
because of how germs make him so sick so fast.
So, for months and months we stayed at home.
No movies. No football games. No restaurants.

Well, except sometimes
when Mom and Dad stayed with Levi
and I could go out with José
to the gross old mall
and we'd go to Game Space
so we could try out the new Halo
until the manager would yell at us
for being there too long and
getting pizza grease on the controllers.
Once we snuck into this movie
and that one actor said every swear
and José thought we were going to get in
so
much
trouble
*Timothy*
*we*
*are*
*dead*
*if*
*we*
*get*
*caught.*

26

But we didn't get caught.
It was so much fun.
You know what?
Now that I think about it?
House arrest stinks.
Like way more than I thought
before I started writing this.
Stupid journal.

✳

Levi can't talk.
You know that already.
But it's not that he just lies around and doesn't
do anything;
he still cries and laughs.
You just can't hear it.
If you think about something that's so funny you
laugh and laugh
until you can't make a noise
and so you sort of suck in air and make a clacking
noise
with your tongue
and a kind of wheeze with your breath,

that's what Levi sounds like when he laughs.
When he cries his face gets all screwed up in a knot,
big tears roll down his cheeks,
and wet bursts come from the tube in his neck.
He hisses, I guess, like a cartoon snake,
or a deflating balloon with lots of slobber in it.
He gets so mad and can't make a noise.
I want to make the noises for him
because it isn't fair, you know?
You should be able to scream
when you need to scream.

❋

Mac and cheese for dinner
again
Peanut butter but no bread
again
powdered milk in stale cereal
again
going to sleep hungry
again

✸

If Levi has to have a nurse all day, every day,
and all night, every night,
then why does he have Marisol only twice a week?
I am not a nurse.
Mom is not a nurse.
We do our best.
But we need sleep.
Mom needs to work.
I need better excuses not to do my homework,
like a real kid:
*I was playing Xbox.*
*My dog ate it.*
*I forgot.*
Not:
*My brother has no nurse, again.*
I like Marisol, though.
When she's here.
It's not her fault when she's not here.
There are other sick kids, too.
And not enough nurses.
But still.

# WEEK 7

James says there are no rules for this journal.
That is more confusing than a wide receiver
*throwing* a pass, James.
(If I talk in football language, Mrs. B,
maybe James will understand more of my words.)
For weeks it has been:
*Talk more about that day, Timothy.*
*Tell us how you feel, Timothy.*
*Make sure we know you're not a nutjob, Timothy.*
And now it's *There are no rules*?
Grown-ups are the worst.

✳

I hear these little noises.
Sniffs and sad chirps.
A hiccup.
A blowing nose.
Mom is crying downstairs.

*

I made her cry, OK.
I made her cry
after I took the family photos off the mantel.
I made her cry
when I threw the pictures out the door and in the yard.
I made her cry
when I yelled, *He left us and he's never coming back
EVER!*
I said I was sorry after she stopped crying.
I picked the pictures up out of the yard.
I put them in the trunk of the car
with the rest of his stuff I'm hiding in there.
José came by on his bike,
asked me why I was talking  to the car.
So I admitted it to him.
I made my mom cry.
It was me this time.
Not a bill.
Not Levi.
Not just from being so, so tired.
I admit it to you, too.

I made her cry, OK.

And then I apologized

to a bunch of photos and stuff in the trunk of our car.

Because I didn't want Dad to hate me.

Maybe I *am* a nutjob.

Oh, great, now I'm crying, too.

I hate this journal.

✳

A crackle in the breeze.

I put down my math book,

look out the front door.

Two bags on the mat,

a mat that says *Fo shizzle welcome to our hizzle,*

a mat Dad bought because he thought it was funny,

a mat Mom hates but won't throw away.

Two bags on the mat.

Filled with milk and bread and cheese and meat

and even some Snickers bars.

I look down the sidewalk.

No one's around.

I bring the mystery bag inside.

Levi kicks his happy leg.

# WEEK 8

I wasn't in juvie very long,
just there to be
processed
and
judged.
But it felt like ages
eons
eternities
stars imploded and were reborn
new planets formed
there was a supernova of shame
growing inside me
and I thought maybe rays of blinding light
would shoot from my fingers
as they were pressed onto the fancy inkless pad
and my fingerprints
joined the other galaxies of whorls and swirls
trapped in time.

✸

*You look cold.*
Duh, Mrs. B. It's wintertime.
*Where's your coat?*

Duh, Mrs. B. My arms have grown
three sizes since last winter.
*Do you need a coat?*
Duh, Mrs. B. But you think I'm going to ask for one?
*You should take care of yourself.*
*You don't want to get sick.*
Duh, Mrs. B. Who *wants* to get sick?
*Have you had a flu shot?*
Duh, Mrs. B. Who's going to pay for it?
*You should think about getting one.*
Duh, Mrs. B. I think about a lot of things I can't do.
*Timothy, are you listening to me?*
Duh, Mrs. B. Are *you* listening to you?

✳

*My mom is late.*
*She'll be right here.*
My standard lie for new night nurses.
Mom will be here when her shift ends.
In three hours.
This nurse plopped down a Big Gulp
right on Mom's coffee table.

The one that should have a sign:
USE A COASTER
OR YOU WILL BE MURDERED.
*Wow. Lexi is adorable. She's a cutie.*
I smelled cigarettes and onions
when she opened her mouth.
*Actually, she's a he.*
*And his name is Levi.*
Onion Mouth wrinkled her nose,
flipped through some pages,
sipped her Big Gulp.
*Oh, right. The heart kid.*
I shook my head.
*Airway kid.* I pointed to the trach.
Onion Mouth smiled.
*Where's your bathroom?*
I pointed down the hall.
Then I called Mom.
*Forget the overtime.*
*Please come home.*
*You have to fire the new night nurse.*
*I know.*

*I know.*
*But she's bad.*
*Real bad.*
*OK.*
*Sorry.*
*I know.*
*I KNOW.*
*Bye.*

✱

**Marisol has these crazy fingers.**
They're long,
like longer than normal.
And they wrap around things,
like maybe she has vines growing inside her.
This afternoon her fingers were twirling
crazy shapes
in front of Levi's face.
She's teaching him sign language.
She's giving him a voice.
*milk milk milk*
*more more more*
*more milk more milk more milk*

Marisol said it over and over
while her fingers curled,
vines squeezing air.
Levi stared at her
and smiled
and swatted at her hands.
Marisol took his hand,
took his tiny fingers
that are not like vines
and she tried to shape them into
*milk milk milk*
*more more more*
*more milk more milk more milk.*
But he just wanted the cell phone
in the pocket of her scrubs.
(He likes to push buttons.
Kind of like me.
Ha.)
I sat next to Marisol
and tried to turn my fingers into vines.
*more more more*
*milk milk milk*
*more milk more milk more milk*

*Good*, said Marisol.
*Good job, Timothy.*
She handed me Levi's bottle.
Her long fingers touched mine
for just a second
and the weirdest thing happened.
I wanted to hug her
really tight
and feel her hands wrap around me
like vines never letting go.
And I wanted to sign
*more more more*
so she'd never stop hugging me back.
Please don't ever tell her.

# WEEK 9

I will never do it again.
You must know that, James.
I will never do it again.
Even though sometimes I wonder
just a tiny wonder
a little piece of dust-sized wonder
miniature wonder
you can only see under a wonderscope.
What if . . .
What if . . .
What if I had one more magic wallet . . .
What if all the bills got paid . . .
I will never do it again, James.
The wonder is very tiny.
The what if is too dangerous.
So I will never do it again.
But I do wonder.
I do.

✹

Hey Dad,
I'm writing this because I have to.
Mrs. Bainbridge is making me write it
in her office
with the plants.
Well, I'm not writing this *with* the plants.
You know what I mean.
Well, no, you don't.
You don't even know Mrs. Bainbridge.
You don't even know why I'm here.
You don't know anything.
Did you ever know anything?
Did you ever think about me?
About Mom?
About Levi?
How *we* feel?
What *we* want?
I guess you only thought about your car
and how fast you would drive it
away, away, away.
I wish *I* could drive
away, away, away.

40

But even if I could, I wouldn't.
Because there are people to take care of.
People you left behind.
I don't want to write this anymore.
Mrs. Bainbridge, there isn't even a place to send it.

✱

You can't hear an angry burrito cry
when that angry burrito
is a baby with a trach
wrapped in a blanket
so that his arms and legs can't move
so that you can bend his neck over a towel
so that you can pull the tube from his neck
and put in a new, clean one.
The angry burrito does not like you
when you help do this,
even when you burrito-ize him
in his favorite spaceship blanket.
Even when you whisper a story about
dragons and a knight
who talks with his hands.
The angry burrito turns weird colors

while your mom and his nurse
work with superfast ninja moves
to get that breathing tube switched out
1-2-3 FAST.
The angry burrito stops crying
when you give him a bottle
pat his fuzzy head
say, *Good job, Levi, good job, little burrito.*
The angry burrito drinks too fast.
The angry burrito barfs and
the ties around his neck
the brand-new ties
get covered in barf
so you have to help switch them out again
and the whole scene starts over
an endless loop
because you have nothing better to do on a Saturday
than make up stories about dragons
to soothe an angry burrito.

✴

Confession:
I ran to José's house today,
just for three minutes
to borrow his math book.
Mom knew where I was going.
She watched from the doorway.
But now I can't think about math.
I can only think about other dimensions
like maybe right now our world exists somewhere else,
but everyone has bunny ears
or their butts on the fronts of their bodies.
When I go to José's house it's like another dimension.
The house is exactly the same as mine,
same rooms in the same places
except it is also exactly different.
They have seven people,
we have three.
They have noise and chaos,
we do too.
But it's just all so different,
so different.

It's hard for me to figure out
who has the best chaos—
Beeping alarms, or screeching sisters?
Backpacks everywhere, or medical supplies?
Fuzzy baby head, or guinea pig running loose?
And all of it,
*all of it* is hidden behind the same-looking front door,
the same-looking windows,
the same-looking garage.
A whole different dimension.
It's just three houses down.
And the only real thing we share
between the two places
is this one lousy math book
that I can't even concentrate on.

✳

José's dad bought a car.
It's a car he says used to be cool.
Now it looks like a giant rusted turtle
with no guts inside.

✹

*T-man, you can't keep doing this.*
The box drops at my feet.
*Don't call me T-man.*
A bobblehead falls next to my foot.
I don't crush it.
*I need the trunk for groceries.*
Her hands on her hips.
Her jaw clenching.
*Put this stuff away.*
The toe of my shoe pushes at the box.
Football. Shaving cream. Random Dad stuff.
I imagine it on fire.
I imagine it on fire in an ocean of lava.
I imagine it on fire in an ocean of lava
with fireproof sharks circling it.
I imagine it on fire in an ocean of lava
with fireproof sharks circling it
and shooting it with their laser eyes.
*There are never any groceries to go in the trunk.*
I say it quietly. To the box.
Levi starts coughing.
Mom goes to him.

When I kick the box, more stuff falls out.
The suction machine is louder than my kicks.
I kick and kick and kick
until Mom stops suctioning
until Levi stops coughing.
Now I'm in my room.
The box is not on fire.
And it's not in the trunk.
And the bobblehead is not in my hand.
And I'm not thinking about Dad.
And how he sucks even more than the suction
machine.

✳

You know those super sunny days?
The ones that come out of nowhere,
where every slant of sunshine
bursts through the window blinds
warming up whatever they touch
not too hot
but just right
and you can feel the sun burning on your face
burning in a good way
like if you could stand inside fireworks and not
get burned?

This fresh-squeezed orange juice
left on the porch
with a box of chocolate doughnuts
and a bag of breakfast tacos
with fiery red salsa
is making the inside of my mouth feel
just like those fireworks
just like that slant of sunshine.

# WEEK 10

I know I can't go to José's house
to help work on the car.
Duh, James.
I was just mentioning it, that's all.
You don't have to always jump down my throat
trying to snatch away my words
like they are bombs about to tear the world apart.
I'm just writing in my journal
like I'm supposed to do.
Jeez.
Do you think every thought I have
is about breaking rules?
Do you think every thought I have
is about how to drive you crazy?
Your squinched-up lips
and grouchy eyebrows
say yes.
Ugh.
Could you be more of a tool?
That is not a challenge.

✹

*Baby Signing Adventure.*
A DVD left on the mat,
seemingly innocent
but like a time bomb
ticking ticking ticking
*MILK MILK MILK*
*in a CUP CUP CUP*
*I LOVE LOVE LOVE*
*My MILK in a CUP.*
*MORE MORE MORE*
*MILK in my CUP*
*I LOVE LOVE LOVE*
*MORE MILK in my CUP.*
Someone left this DVD for Levi
but as a punishment for me,
right?
Because, you guys.
This is worse than juvie.
I am not even kidding.
Five times he's watched this DVD today.
FIVE TIMES.

Happy leg kicking away.
I can almost see the smoke
shooting from his ears
as that little brain of his works and works.
But seriously.
*Baby Signing Adventure* might kill me.
For real.
My ears will bleed from all those songs.
My heart will explode from running
to get away from Miss Jill
and her pointy talking fingers.
But Levi can't get enough.
So thanks.
Whoever left it here.
I guess.

❋

No, Mrs. B.
There is no way
no how
no where
no when
that Mom would ever
in one million years

allow a benefit to raise money
to help us.
Because we don't need help.
We're just like everyone else.
Or so she says.

✳

I got home from school,
Marisol handed me a package.
An envelope with padding.
Can you fit a million dollars
in an envelope with padding?
I opened it and must have given her a look
because she laughed.
*What are these?*
*Chains.*
*I can see that, Marisol.*
*For Levi. Come here. Help me.*
We burrito-ized Levi.
I whispered the story in his ear,
the one about the dragon
and the knight who talks with his fingers.
Marisol unfastened the fabric around his neck,
the ties that hold his trach in place,

the ties that get ten times disgusting

whenever he barfs

or spits out his milk

or sweats

or all of those things combined.

Marisol gently pulled the ties away from the trach,

using her other hand to hold the trach in Levi's neck.

One slip,

one distraction,

and the trach could fall out,

could mean no more breathing for Levi.

*Hand me the chains?*

I handed them over and she measured the perfect fit.

*Cut right here.*

I took the wire cutters from the package.

I cut right there.

Marisol connected the chain through the trach

and around Levi's neck.

*No more yucky ties.*

She smiled.

*So easy to clean.*

I smiled.

*And look at that cute little neck!*

Levi smiled.

OK. So. Not as good as a million dollars.

But close.

✷

There are sharks in my throat.

Tiny sharks.

With supersharp teeth.

With laser eyes.

They are destroying my throat.

From the inside out.

There are trolls in my head.

Evil trolls.

With superheavy hammers.

With thundering fists.

They are destroying my head.

From the inside out.

It's possible I am dying.

Infected with sharks and trolls.

But I have a math test today.

NO REST FOR THE WEARY.

✸

I can hear them downstairs.
Mom has that voice.
The one she uses when she's really mad
but trying to be calm.
I call it her
I Will Kill You, But in a Superpolite Way voice.
Tonight's nurse is getting a face full of
IWKYBIASWV
I hear the words *go-bag* and *organized*
then the fake laugh that is like
IWKYBIASWV's sidekick.
The nurse makes a *pshhh* noise
and I want to yell,
*Jump back, lady!*
*You're about to get murdered with words!*
But I stay at the top of the stairs
listening, listening, listening.
No one messes with the go-bag.
It has everything Levi needs if we have to leave the
house.
Not that he ever does.

Except for doctor visits.

Or emergencies.

The go-bag is a work of art.

Labeled supplies, rescue meds, extra trachs,

even a handheld suction thing.

You don't touch the go-bag.

You don't go near the go-bag.

The go-bag is perfection.

It's like a tiny hospital

in an ugly red duffel.

I think the nurse tried to reorganize it.

MISTAKE.

That go-bag is the most perfect thing

Dad ever created.

Except maybe me. Har.

# WEEK 11

We don't take Levi out a lot
because of the germs, you know?
Sometimes we have to, though.
And that's when we see
Other
People
dun dun duuuuuuun.
First the forehead gets wrinkly,
then the lips turn down in a frown.
the head tilts to the side,
sometimes there's a *tsk*-ing noise
or a sigh and a head shake.
A lot of times there's an "I'm sorry."
But that's dumb.
I mean, come on.
Why are *you* sorry, ugly lady at the grocery store?
Did *you* give Levi a messed-up airway?
Did *you* give him a trach?
No.
That's the one thing I like about you, James.
Maybe the only thing.

You see Levi all the time
And you never say you're sorry.
You wash your hands,
you ruffle his hair,
you soft-punch his tiny baby shoulder
and say, *What's up, sir.*
Did they teach you how to not say you're sorry?
At Probation Officer University, I mean?
Or is that just a James thing?
Either way, thanks.
Thanks for never being sorry, James.

✸

*Should I call social services?*
Mrs. B asked me that.
I thought she meant because I'm quiet,
because my social skills are lacking,
like I need a tutor for learning how to talk to people,
but that's not what she meant.
*If your mom is overwhelmed,*
*if there isn't enough food,*
*if it's not safe for Levi,*
*you can tell me, Timothy.*

*There are people and places who can help.*
And it was like she hit me.
Right in the teeth.
She meant like Family Cops
who can take away babies
and kids
and put them in other people's houses.
So I was like *NO NO NO NO NO!*
And she had to say *OK* a hundred times
and *I'm sorry* a thousand times
and I think maybe her eyes filled up with tears.
It was a little bit crazy.
But not crazy enough for social services.
I swear.

❋

José brought over a crumpled picture.
Take one turtle
shoot it with a ray gun
set to ENLARGE,
remove the turtle's eyes,
replace the turtle's legs with flat tires,
take out all of the turtle's guts,
replace with rusted metal.

This is the car José and his dad are fixing up,
a sad and busted turtle
who somehow managed to save his shell
but nothing else.
*How am I supposed to know*
*what a stupid seal puller looks like?*
*What do you do when your dad yells at you*
*for no reason at all?*
The question came out of his mouth
before he realized what he was saying.
I said nothing
but my eyes told him to shut his pie hole.
My eyes told him to get on back home
with his dad and their busted-up turtle car.
So he did.
And now I feel kind of bad.
But not that bad.

❋

José is here.
Again.
I'm hiding from him.
In the bathroom.
He just . . .

He never stops talking.
How much he hates his dad.
How much he hates that car.
How much he hates his sisters.
How much he hates his lunch.
I just want to punch him in the mouth.
Hard.
At least you can hate your dad to his face.
At least you have time to spend together.
At least your sisters breathe through their noses.
At least you have a decent lunch.
I take back feeling bad yesterday,
when I was grouchy with him.
He just doesn't even know.
Has zero clues.
About anything.
At least he brought his math book over.
He might not know anything about anything
but at least he remembers to bring his books
home from school
and at least he knows all the x- and y-axis stuff.
Freakin' José.

# WEEK 12

*What's the story with your face?*
You have to work on your social skills, James.
What's the story with my face?
It's filled with sharks and trolls and snot and fire.
And now my neck and my knees and my elbows hurt.
But at least I don't have a trach, right?
I can't really complain about
the story my face is telling.
It's just a cold.
I'm fine.

❀

You'd think maybe I have the black plague
the way Mrs. B sucked in her breath
when she saw me this morning.
*I'm fine.*
*It's just a cold.*
She shook her head.
Her hair swished.
I don't think I've ever seen her hair down before.
You almost look like a movie star, Mrs. B.

Except with more lines around your eyes.
No offense.
She handed me a card.
People's Clinic.
*Go get checked out, Timothy.*
*Your mom can even take you after work.*
*This place is open nice and late.*
I shrugged.
I didn't say:
*No nurse tonight.*
*No one to watch Levi.*
*No way we can bring him with us.*
Maybe I should have.
It doesn't matter, though.
I'm fine.
It's just a cold.

*

I hate wearing a mask.
It's already hard to breathe
and the mask makes it worse.
I've been trying to stay upstairs.
Keeping my germs in their own galaxy far, far away.

But sometimes Mom or Marisol still need my help.
On her way out the door
Marisol called up to me.
I staggered downstairs.
The zombie formerly known as Timothy.
She pressed a box in my hand.
Pills.
For the flu.
*They're from last year, but still good.*
*Take them, Timothy. Get better, sport.*
I hate it when she calls me *sport.*
But I took the pills.
Even though it's just a cold.

✸

The sharks and trolls are battling inside me.
Marisol's pills might actually be working.
Maybe.
I sat with Levi today.
Wearing my mask.
Sanitizing my hands.
The first day in a long time
we could kind of hang out.

I used my short fingers
to sign *brother*
over and over
and to fold his shorter fingers
to sign *brother*
over and over.
*Brother*
I patted my chest
then showed him the sign.
Levi fussed and cried.
*Brother*
I patted his chest
then showed him the sign again.
Levi fussed and cried.
*Brothers*
I folded my fingers
and folded his fingers.
He pushed away my hands.
He cried.
He needed suctioning.
He felt warm.
He refused his milk.

Oh, little brother.
Was I hiding from you for too long?
Or are you getting sick?

*

please don't have him be getting sick
please don't have him be getting sick
please don't have him be getting sick
please don't have him be getting sick
please don't have him be getting sick

# WEEK 13

*Did you make it yourself?*
I couldn't help but take a step back.
The thought of James in a kitchen,
the thought of James giving a grouchy look to carrots
because they weren't cutting themselves into the
right shapes.
*I bought it.*
*You should eat it.*
*Chicken soup is like medicine*
*There are studies.*
I said, *OK.*
And took it.
And felt relief for those carrots.

✳

Sometimes I shake
like a little earthquake that is only inside of me.
It happens when I talk about That Day.
It happens when I talk about Levi.
It happens when I think about Dad.
It happens when I think about any day
that's not today.

Sometimes it happens when I *do* think about today.
But yesterday, I did not shake.
Mrs. B sat me on that squishy couch
and she put a pillow on my head.
I was like, *What?*
but she smiled and said, *Trust me*
so I squinted my eyes
because you never trust an adult
when they say *trust me.*
But I didn't move.
Next, she put a weird heavy pillow on my arm.
And another one on my other arm.
The last thing she did,
and this was the craziest thing of all,
she put a bowling ball in my lap.
A real bowling ball.
And she stared at me all serious-like
with pillows on my arms
and on my head
and a bowling ball in my lap
and she said, *What do you think?*
I couldn't even answer
because for the first time since Levi was born
I could talk about things without shaking.

How do pillows and a bowling ball make you feel calm?
Beats me.
But they did.
It was so nice, I could have stayed that way all day
and all night
just stuck there on that couch
anchored
still
safe
looking like a complete dummy
but not shaking,
And almost even relaxed.
I hope I didn't get any germs on anything.

✳

I got germs on something.
Even with all the washing
and the hand sanitizer
and wearing a mask
like a doctor
whenever I come near Levi,
I still got germs on something.

Marisol just went home.
She had a line between her eyes.
The worried line.
She'll be back in the morning.
We just have to get to the morning.
*He'll be fine*, she said.
The worried line did not go away.

\*

Four stoplights, plus
one stop sign, plus
one parking place (superhard to find).
That's all it takes
to get to the hospital.
But it feels like
four thousand years, plus
one eternity, plus
one frozen car door (superhard to open).
That's all it takes
to get to the hospital.
Forever or ten minutes?
Sometimes they're the same, aren't they?

✳

Running. We were running.
Mom was ahead of me
slap slap slap slap
her feet bare, the hallway empty
except for Levi
on the speeding gurney
just like a TV show.
A nurse was riding with him
holding the ambu bag over his trach
squeezing squeezing squeezing,
and a different nurse said, in a rushed voice:
*You have to stay out here.*
*We'll find you when he's stabilized.*
Then they were through the doors
at the end of the hall,
the sign shouted INTENSIVE CARE in all caps
but that was the only shouting.
Mom's elbows were on her knees,
her back moving up and down up and down
but she wasn't breathing hard from running.
She was crying.

Crying so hard.
Like I've never seen.
And I just stood there
holding the go-bag like an idiot.
The place was empty
neither one of us could move.
All of our energy
had been sucked away
through the doors at the end of the hall.
So we sat
right there on the floor
and Mom cried into my shoulder
and she made noises I've never heard before
like an animal in a trap, maybe,
and we waited to hear something
anything
but we didn't hear anything for a long time
only those shouting words on the doors
INTENSIVE CARE INTENSIVE CARE
and we were the only two people in the world
sitting in that hallway.
Still. Right there on the floor.

With the walls crashing down around us
even as they glowed under the barely buzzing
bright lights.

*

Mom is finally asleep.
The nice nurse threatened to clonk her on the head
and knock her out.
Instead, Mom took a pill.
She's asleep in the chair,
her head on the rail of Levi's bed.
She doesn't want me to call anyone.
She never wants to ask for help.
But I could call José's mom.
She could bring clothes.
Mom's shoes.
And maybe snacks.
Don't you think it's OK
to cry uncle sometimes?
To ask for help?
Otherwise you're just crying.
And how does that help anyone?
I'm going to call José's mom.

I'm going to do it.
We need help.
I don't care what Mom says.

＊

I don't know what to do.
I'm lost.
I'm lost.
He's so sick.

卌 卌 卌 卌 卌

卌 卌 卌 卌 卌

卌 卌 卌 卌 卌

卌 卌 卌 卌 卌

# SPRING

# WEEK 14

*It's been fourteen weeks.*
He says it like I don't know.
*Fourteen weeks, Timothy.*
*How are you holding up?*
I look over at him.
His face more scruff than beard.
His dark eyes, staring.
His hair blowing in the breeze.
Too young to be Dad's age,
Too old to be cool.
I shrug.
*Aren't we past shrugging?*
He doesn't smile
but his face isn't hard, either.
Not like it used to be.
We're sitting outside
in the hospital courtyard.
It's sunny today,
almost warm.
*You want some lunch?*
*I have an extra half.*

He pulls a sandwich from his bag.
It's cut into thirds.
An *extra half*? Really?
James, I think you are worse at math than me.

✳

Still in ICU.
Still watching machines breathe for Levi.
It was just a cold.
Just a cold.

✳

She seems really nice.
Her hand pushes the hair from Levi's forehead
and she makes sure *Baby Signing Adventure*
plays in the background
even though he's pretty out of it.
This morning, though,
when Mom was down the hall in the shower,
this nurse,
this nice lady with tired eyes
and painted eyebrows,
she said, *Supposably, the doctor will be here soon.*

*Supposably* is not a word.
Can you keep a baby alive
if you are kind
and you have tired eyes
but you don't know that *supposably* isn't a real word?
José would call me a jerk
for being picky and weird
but I'm just saying . . .
How do you know?
If someone can keep a baby alive?
How do you ever know?

❇

José's mom was not having it.
*You listen to me, Annie.*
*That boy is just a boy.*
*He needs rest. Food.*
*He needs to be a boy.*
*I'm taking him with me.*
*The judge, the court, they can take it up with me.*
Her mouth was in a tight line
but then it softened.
*Just for tonight, Annie.*
*Just for tonight.*

The last part she said like she was soothing
a hurt animal.
Her face crinkled into a quiet smile.
I stayed peeking behind the hospital room's
bathroom door.
José's mom put her hand on Mom's shoulder.
She leaned down and whispered:
*You need a break,* Mami.
Her hand squeezed.
*How about I take you* both *tomorrow night?*
Mom laid her cheek on José's mom's hand.
Mom closed her eyes.
Swallowed hard.
Not crying.
Almost crying.
A machine alarmed and the nurse came in.
I put my bag over my shoulder.
Walked out of the bathroom.
José's mom put her other hand on my shoulder.
We all looked at Levi as the nurse checked the alarm.
*Let's go,* mijo.
She steered me to the door.
I stopped to look at Mom.
Should I leave her?

It's against the rules of house arrest.
And what about Levi? What if something happens?
*Levi is in safe hands*, José's mom whispered.
She turned to Mom and smiled her soft smile again.
*Don't worry,* Mami.
*Timothy is in safe hands, too.*

✳

You know how when you shake a snow globe
everything swirls around?
José's house is like that.
On the outside it looks like a plain, regular house.
On the inside everything is moving, swirling,
talking, laughing.
Theresa flies through the room,
soccer cleats over her shoulder
yelling about being late to practice.
Sofia drops a glass and it shatters on the tile,
she swears and starts to clean up the mess
never taking off her headphones
never not dancing.
Alé is upstairs
oomPAH oomPAH oomPAH

playing the tuba
and making the whole thing seem like a TV show.
Isa swings her backpack to the floor,
*thud.*
Her hair falls around her face
a black curtain.
And when she smiles it's like the curtain opens.
And the light shines bright
so bright
it kind of hurts my eyes.
It may be very possible
the only thing in this crazy snow globe
that's not moving right now
is me.

❊

Isa is at the table with us,
four books open
one in her lap
her glasses on her head, holding her hair back.
She looks up.
*What are you writing, Timothy?*
*Nothing.*

My face is suddenly five hundred degrees.

She smiles,

then frowns.

*Have you seen my glasses?*

Her hands pass over the table,

she looks on the floor.

*On your head,* gordita, José says with a snort.

Now Isa's face turns red.

I punch José in the arm.

Just a playful punch.

But Isa gathers up her books and goes upstairs.

She walks in rhythm to Alé's

oomPAH oomPAH music

but not on purpose.

I think.

# WEEK 15

It's kind of soothing after a while,
the beep beep beeping.
The machines measuring Levi's life.
A nonstop rhythm.
Even when he's not moving
and has all those wires on him
and all that medicine pumping into him,
we hear beep beep beeping.
Heartbeats turned into heartbeeps.
So we always know
he's still alive.

❋

José's mom and James and Mom are talking
in the hallway.
James looks pale.
He really hates hospitals.
I almost feel bad for him.
Almost.
I am *doing homework* while they talk
which of course means

*listening to everything they say*
I hear
*grades*
*responsibility*
*I know*
*good kid*
*judge's approval*
and other stuff.
José's mom wants me to start sleeping at their house.
Not permanent,
but while Levi is in the hospital.
Also, she wants me there for dinners.
I want to do it.
But I don't want to do it.
What will Mom do without me?
Who will remind her to eat?

❋

I am in José's family's giant van.
Heading to see Mrs. B.
It is just as crazy as the house.
Soccer bag, dance bag, music stand, books.

Yelling, talking, laughing, shoving.
Every corner of the van
has something or someone stuffed into it.
José's mom is singing loud and proud
to some song with a thumping beat.
Everyone is acting like her voice is a weapon
killing them, ears first.
She is laughing and singing,
the van driving through a storm.
I just hold on tight,
fingers gripping my seat belt.
It's like the world is swallowing me
one laugh at a time.
Isa cracks José on the head with a book.
Can I laugh while Levi is so sick?
Can I be happy with Mom so scared?
The rain streaks across the windows.
*We are almost there,* mijo.
José's mom runs her fingers through her hair
while the van is stopped at a red light.
She turns back to smile at me.
*Almost there.*

✻

Be creative.

The teachers at school say that all the time.

Having trouble solving a problem?

Be creative.

Having trouble writing an essay?

Be creative.

Having trouble keeping your brother alive?

Be creative.

Well, they don't say that last one.

It's true, though, you know.

I bet if the doctors were more creative

Levi would get better.

*All the way* better.

Mom says they're doing their best.

She says we're on Levi time, just like always.

But you know what?

That doesn't mean we can't be creative.

Having trouble listening to your mom?

Be creative.

*

*Subglottic stenosis.*
*Bronchiectasis.*
*Failure to Thrive.*
I copied those words down from Levi's chart.
I don't know how to say most of them,
or even what they mean.
Well, I can kind of guess at the last one,
but it doesn't seem like a sickness.
It seems like a judgment.
I'm going to look them up,
because I don't believe,
not for one second,
that Levi has to live like this every day.
There has to be something we can do.
Someone we can call.

*

I need a computer.
There's only one at José's house
and someone is always on it.

The one at my house hasn't had the Internet
in months and months.
School has a ton.
But I have no free time to use them.
What do you think, Mrs. B?
Can I use your computer?
I know the plants won't mind.
Will you?

# WEEK 16

James has on his Serious Face.
His Probation Officer University face.
*Mr. and Mrs. Jimenez have been interviewed*
*and approved.*
*The judge respects the situation.*
Mom talks to him like a robot.
*Yes, no, yes, I understand.*
Her eyes are stuck to Levi.
Like he's her sun instead of just her son,
like she's a glob of plasma
reaching and stretching to him.
She gets her energy from knowing he's right there.
She can't not touch him.
*You worry about Levi.*
*We have Timothy under control.*
We have Timothy under control.
Like I am a disease.

✳

James is pale again.
He's out of breath, like he's run to the hospital.
But I don't think he's done any running.
I think it's true:

he really
really
really
hates hospitals.
Now I know your kryptonite, James.
Now I know if we have all our meetings at the hospital
you will forget to yell at me,
all your power lost
to fear
of beeps
and sick babies
and stinging smells.

＊

Mrs. B.
Long blond hair,
it's almost like a lion's mane.
Sharp eyes.
Green one day, gray the next,
almost never blinking.
She doesn't look like a devil
but I *feel* like I've made a deal with one.
(Does that count as talking about my feelings?)
Her computer is free for me to use.

She'll even help me print stuff,
but only if I talk about my feelings first.
Only if we can have a *dialogue* first.
Yeah. A deal with the devil.
The green-eyed devil.

✹

*Take this one.*
*And this one.*
*And these.*
*And this.*
José's mom is throwing piles of clothes at me.
José is in the garage working on the turtle car
with his dad.
*You are so skinny,* mijo.
*These are all from two years ago*
*but I think they will fit.*
A pile of clothes builds up at my feet
like a snowdrift of José, the First Generation.
There's no way I can say no to these clothes.
No way José's mom will *let* me say no.
So I gather them up,
like the ghosts of winters past,
and already, I feel warmer.

＊

José's mom took me to the hospital
and when we went into Levi's room
Mom was asleep
Levi was asleep
it was dark and quiet
except for the
heartbeeps
and the nurse popped her head in the door
a grocery bag in her hand.
*Timothy? Someone left this for you.*
Inside the bag:
two new toothbrushes
candy bars
bananas
nonslip socks
a magazine about movie stars
a magazine about video games
a *Baby Signing Adventure* book.
*Who is it from?*
The nurse just shrugged,
smiled,
closed the door.

\*

Levi is feeling much better!
Maybe just one more week.
If we don't jinx it.
And then he'll be home.
And I'll be home.
No more IV tubes.
No more doctors and pokes.
No more hospital.
No more fancy home-cooked dinners.
No more José and Theresa and Sofia and Alé.
No more Isa.
How should I feel about that?
I don't know how to feel about that.

\*

Books on the table
pencils scribbling
oomPAH oomPAH
José telling me
hurry hurry hurry up with your homework
so we can play Halo.
Yummy smells coming from the kitchen,

Isa tapping her fingers on her nose
counting syllables
or maybe integers.
Everyone busy
but no wild eyes.
Then a key in the door,
shuffling shoes.
José's mom shouts something from the kitchen,
José's dad loosening his tie,
dropping his briefcase.
Isa stands and hugs him.
José tells about the math test and how well he did.
The oomPAHing stops and Alé flies down the stairs.
They are a crowd
even with Theresa and Sofia not at home.
They are all talking at once.
José's dad acts annoyed as he tries to get
to the kitchen
but he's smiling.
José's mom steps into the dining room
wipes her hands on her apron
kisses him big on the mouth
and I am still at the table
alone

feeling suddenly itchy to not be here
in this house
but I can't be anywhere else
and José's dad says over the noise,
*Timothy*,
and he nods at me
and I nod back
swallowing a rock in my throat
wondering why everything just got so weird.

# WEEK 17

I know everything will be back to normal soon.
I am not a moron, James.
I *know* it will not be José's house all the time.
I *know* it will not be José's mom taking me places.
I *know* it will be back to business as usual.
You don't have to talk to me like I'm an idiot.
James.
Mrs. B.
School.
Mom.
I will be back in the house arrest box.
I mean, it's not like I really left it,
I just had little tunnels
like those tunnels hamsters get to run around in.
Those tunnels can stretch across a whole room,
even up toward the ceiling
where the little hamster runs and runs.
But in the end?
All tunnels lead right back to the cage.
So don't worry, James.
I get it.
Back to normal soon.
Fine.

✹

Look who's on his wedge
dangling like a wiggly booger.
Cutest booger I've ever seen.
Marisol is humming and signing,
Levi waves his hands
without actually signing anything.
I can tell, though.
He's happy to be home.
So happy.

✹

*What is THIS?*
Mom shrieks in the kitchen.
I knew she would.
But I also know she won't give anything back.
Tamales, enchiladas,
frozen containers of *borracho* beans,
some kind of cake.
José's mom.
She made us dinner for every night this week.
I gave her my key so she could sneak inside
and fill up the empty freezer
while I was at school
and Mom got Levi home from the hospital.

*We can't accept this*, Mom says
while she eats a cold tamale.
*Definitely not*, I say, taking one,
sprinkling masa crumbs down my shirt.
*We should totally give these back*, I say,
reaching for another.
Mom laughs for the first time in a long time.
She puts frozen beans in the microwave.
*We really shouldn't accept this*, she says again,
eating a corn bread muffin.
*Definitely not*, I repeat
The microwave beeps
and we don't even get bowls
we just eat the beans right out of the container.

❋

*Nominate a charity!*
Mrs. B.
Really.
Come on.
Where did you get this?
*Who deserves a Carnival of Giving?*
Mrs. B.
Seriously.
Um, A) My family is not a charity
and 2) Mom would never say yes.

Not in a hundred million years.
*Nominations for next year's Carnival start TODAY!*
By next year
we could all be flattened by an asteroid
or destroyed by a zombie plague.
I mean, you don't know.
How can you plan for next year
when tomorrow seems like
a hundred years away?
P.S. Don't rip flyers off the middle school walls.
That is super creepy.
FYI

✳

Here's the thing with school, overall:
It exists.
It's a thing.
I go to it.
I come home.
I don't love it.
I don't hate it.
It feels like a giant mountain just—
BAM
right in the middle of the road
slowing down the rest of my life
in a super annoying kind of way.

I can't get over it, because it's too . . . much.
Unmoving.
Unmoved.
Unmoveable.
And the only way around it
is to carve a tunnel through it,
through dirt and crap in every direction
trying to maybe find something useful along the way
but mostly just getting annoyed
because there seems to be no end to the tunnel
or the crap
that just goes on
forever and forever and forever.

# WEEK 18

*What are you feeling today, Timothy?*
Mrs. B asks this every week.
Not *how* are you feeling, Timothy, but *what* are
you feeling.
I am feeling José's shirt on my back.
I am feeling my toes pressed against the tips
of my shoes.
I am feeling the squishy couch under my butt.
I am feeling the breeze from the vent
blowing down my neck.
I am feeling the broken pencil in my pocket.
I am feeling the itch of a zit on my nose.
I am feeling the growl in my stomach because
it's past lunch
and not quite dinnertime.
But what do I say?
*I feel nothing, Mrs. B.*
*I feel nothing.*

✳

Feeling nothing doesn't earn me time on the
computer.
You know how *that* makes me *feel*?
Sad
Mad
Tired
Grouchy
Frustrated
Those are not dwarves.
They are *feelings*, OK?
They are like nickels and quarters
jangling, jangling, jangling
buying me time on Mrs. B's computer.

✳

*What are you looking for?*
Mrs. B's hair slides around off her shoulder
trapping her face next to mine
trapping us in a corner
trapping me until I answer.
*A doctor.*

She doesn't say anything.
I feel the warmth of her face
near my face.
I smell her perfume or shampoo
that somehow smells tired.
I type *subglottic stenosis*
and click search.
Mrs. B writes something down.
She slides a piece of paper toward me.
*Subglottic stenosis pediatric doctor*
I type in the extra words.
There are 35,600 results.
So many links.
Mrs. B stands up
her hair slides back into place.
For one second her hand touches my shoulder
then she moves away.
35,600 results.
That's a lot of doctors, right?
I suddenly feel a lot less trapped.
By everything.

✳

Yeah.
35,600 is not the number of doctors
who fix broken babies,
it's just a bunch of studies
and hospitals
and things that have nothing to do with anything.
Uuugh.
Now what?

✳

Mystery bag contents for the week:
Bread
Milk
Cheese
Bologna
Spaghetti
Sauce
Vanilla yogurt
Frozen OJ
And in a second mystery bag:
popcorn kernels
butter
an action movie DVD

with the $4.99 sticker still on it.
When I picked up the bag
off the mat
I looked down the street
like I always do
and this time
this time
I saw something.
A red car turning by the stop sign.
The same color red as James's car.

✻

Mom and I are watching the movie
upstairs
alone
with popcorn
in her bed!
It's so weird
hearing the suction machine downstairs
and knowing Levi is down there
but that we're up here.
Every time I hear it I jump
but Mom's hand goes to my knee.
*He's fine*, she smiles.

*Let's have some you-and-me time, OK?*
*OK.*
I should be used to night nurses by now,
but we hardly ever get one scheduled.
It's nice.
But weird.
I better put this notebook down
before I get butter all over it.

*

Are you leaving these bags, James?
Has it been you the whole time?
Even at the hospital?
Because I know how much you hate hospitals.
It must have been hard
to show up there anyway
and pay to park
and go inside
and get buzzed into the ICU
and stay hidden from us
and give a bag to a nurse
and ask her to give it to us.
I mean, that's a lot of stuff to do
when you're scared of a place.

Our breath must have been really bad
for you to go to all that trouble
to get us new toothbrushes.
*If* it was you leaving the bags.
It might not have been.
I don't know.
Leaving bags of cool stuff . . .
that doesn't seem like a
Probation Officer University thing.
That seems like just a nice person thing.

# WEEK 19

*We'll find the money.*
Mom was talking to herself.
*We'll find a way.*
Her face leaning forward,
her hands in her hair,
papers all over the kitchen table.
She didn't see me
so I snuck back upstairs.

✳

The Carnival of Giving.
I'm thinking about it.
Thinking about that stupid flyer
Mrs. B stole from school.
The one still crumpled up on my desk,
the one I can't quite throw away.
Mom would never say yes.
I can't help but wonder . . .
No.
It's stupid.

❋

We're fine.

Please don't worry.

It's not like we live in a cave in China.

Or in a hut in Africa.

It's not like there are flies circling my face.

Or clods of dirt caked on my feet.

We have enough.

We're OK.

Please, Mrs. B, don't talk about social services again.

We're doing our best.

We're fine.

❋

*What is that, T-man?*

*Don't call me T-man.*

I held up the bag so Mom could see inside.

I couldn't help smiling.

Thick-cut bacon

sourdough bread

eggs

syrup

a cactus with a pink flower
and a pair of tiny socks
exactly Levi's size.
I know it's you, James.
Only you could give things
prickly and soft
sweet and sour
all at the same time.

*

*You and that journal, Timothy*
Isa sat next to me at lunch, smiled,
made my head go all sunny.
I didn't know she had B lunch.
My cheeks went red from the sun in my brain.
*I have to keep the journal. Court-ordered.*
(You know, when she nods, her hair shines extra shiny
like she must have sun in her head, too,
shining through.)
*What are you doing here,* gordita?
José dropped his tray next to mine
splattering spaghetti sauce
making Isa jump back and scowl.
*I'm tutoring during C lunch.*
*Maybe you should skip lunch.*
Then he puffed out his cheeks and laughed.

I really wish he wouldn't do things like that.

She's his sister, fine.

But still.

Isa stood up, no bites taken from her lunch.

*See you later, Timothy.*

She turned, and was gone.

My cheeks still red, but now for a different reason.

✳

*How goes the turtle?*

*Huh?*

*The car? How's it going? With your dad?*

*Oh. Fine.*

*Are you, like, bonding and stuff?*

*I don't know.*

*He's not teaching you the meaning of life?*

*I don't know. Mostly he yells at me a lot.*

*Oh.*

*Yeah.*

*Thanks for the food.*

*I just brought it over. But you're welcome.*

*Bye.*

*Bye.*

José is acting weird.

# WEEK 20

We were laughing so hard,
so hard that no sound was coming out.
Me and Mom
laughing and laughing
because the birthday candle wouldn't stand up
in the pile of vanilla yogurt
in the blue bowl
on Levi's tray.
It would pitch one way
and then the other
and Mom would scream and laugh
as she tried to get it upright
and not burn her fingers.
I thought Levi was laughing, too,
at first,
maybe trying to blow out the candle
with puffs of air from his neck.
But he wasn't laughing or puffing,
he was choking.
We were laughing,
not noticing
until he turned blue

and Mom swore
yanking him from his high chair
throwing him on the couch
ripping the emergency trach from where we leave it
taped to the wall.
I held him down,
she swapped out the trachs,
suctioned and suctioned and suctioned
gave him oxygen puffs from the big tank
until his eyes cleared
his smile woke up
his little hands signed *more more more*.
And that is the story of Levi's first birthday.
I think, actually, it is kind of perfect.

✹

*We need more help.*
The words slip out between my teeth
like mud dripping from fingers.
Slow. Uncontrolled.
drip
plop
splat
Mrs. B looks up.

She's trying not to look surprised
but her forehead gives her away.
One line between her eyes
for each word out of my mouth.
She puts down her pen.
Her eyes hold my eyes
like two tractor beams.
*What kind of help?*
Her voice is very quiet
like maybe I'm a squirrel
and she's trying to feed me an acorn
from the palm of her hand.
Come closer, little squirrel.
Closer.
Closer.
*We need a nurse every day*, I say.
*Every day and every night.*
Mrs. B nods. She writes something down.
She looks up.
Good job, little squirrel.
Good job.
Mrs. B puts her other hand on my hand.
I don't pull it away.

✸

A soft knock.
Can't be the mailman.
He bangs.
Can't be the medical supply delivery guy.
He was here last week.
Another soft knock.
Maybe it's a million-dollar delivery.
I open the door.
*Hi, Timothy.*
Hands holding a covered dish
stacked with another covered dish
and a small paper bag on the tippy-top—
black hair shines
black glasses slipping down her nose
she peeks around the pile of food
she smiles and looks away.
My face feels warm.
*Hi, Isa.*
*Mami sent dinner.*
But I don't hear her words.
I only see her fingertips
wrapped around the dishes,

her nails painted with stars.
Little yellow stars.
A whole unknown universe
on each small finger.

✺

Maybe I would ask Dad
for advice about girls
but probably not
though you never know
not like I need advice
about girls
I mean
I'm just saying.
Never mind.

✺

At school today
I caught myself,
like actually stopped in my tracks
in the hallway outside of gym,
and put both hands over my mouth.
I was humming the theme song to
*Baby Signing Adventure*
and I was liking it.

# WEEK 21

*How big are your feet?*
I thought you were speaking in code, James.
That's why I didn't answer.
Not at first.
I was deciphering your code.
*How big are your feet?*
You mean for running from crimes committed?
*How big are your feet?*
You mean, will I be tall enough
to beat you up one day?
*How big are your feet?*
For stomping and pitching fits?
But you meant it just like you asked it.
How big are my feet.
Then you plopped down the sneakers.
Not new, but almost new.
*Check out these kicks.*
And you thought you were so cool
saying kicks instead of sneakers.
James. James. James.
But you got the size exactly right.
Did you used to work at a carnival?
Now *that* would be cool.

(Thanks for the sneakers.)
(I mean kicks.)
(Well, no, I don't. I mean sneakers.)
(Ha.)

❋

*What do you think about*
*when you think about your father?*
Mrs. B sounds so formal
when she asks questions like that.
*What do I think about?*
I look at the phone on Mrs. B's desk.
It's rectangular and flat,
shiny and smooth,
sometimes it vibrates or beeps
and she ignores it because we're talking
or, really, *she's* talking.
But Dad never ignored his phone
that was also rectangular and flat,
shiny and smooth,
and never far from his hand.
It had games on it
and beeps from doctors and people at work,
and reminders for Levi's appointments.

*This is kind of like the heart of the family,*
he said once
holding it up
as it chirped with messages.
*Everything circulates through this phone.*
*Cool, huh?*
And I said, *Cool.*
And I was so stupid
on the rainy day when he went to the pharmacy
to pick up Levi's meds.
So stupid.
Because I noticed he'd left his phone
right there on the kitchen counter
black and smooth.
He'd left the heart of the family
right there in the open
with nothing but a dying battery.
And I should have known it was a clue.
I should have known
if he could leave the heart of the family
he could leave us, too.
That's what I think about
when I think about my father.
Can I use the computer now?

＊

She thought she was being sneaky,
that I wouldn't notice the picture
back on the wall.
The one with me
and Dad
and a football in the air
frozen in a moment of time
so long ago.
But I noticed.
When she got home from work
and saw the picture,
saw the newly drawn devil horns
and evildoer mustache
and vampire teeth
all on Dad's face . . .
She noticed.
But all she said was
*Fair enough.*
And then we ate dinner
smiling into our spaghetti.

✳

Who is in charge of that Carnival thing?
The Carnival of Giving?
Why does it have such a dumb name?
Why can't it be the
Secretly Put Money in This Envelope Celebration
or the
Congrats, You Won the Fake Lottery Party
or the
Shut Up and Take the Money Fiesta?
I've been to the Carnival before.
The people who are getting the money give speeches
on a stage,
a stage filled with balloons.
They smile and wave
and take all the money back to their
homeless dogs or
nonexistent skate park or
library with not enough books.
I've never seen a family make those speeches.
I've never seen just three people get the money.

I mean, we're not a charity,
so it's not even possible.
I should throw this flyer away.

✳

*They've found us more hours.*
At first I didn't know what Mom meant.
They've found us more hours?
Who?
Wizards?
Scientists?
A secret group of time-pausing elves?
Do we really *need* more hours?
Aren't the days long enough?
Won't we get older faster?
Won't we be *more* tired?
Who actually needs more hours?
*More* nursing *hours, Timothy.*
I smiled, said:
*Maybe Marisol could just move in.*
It was a joke.
But Mom's face crumpled.
It just caved in on itself.
*Marisol can't work full time.*

*The nursing agency will send someone new.*
Wait.
*What?*
*No more Marisol?*
Just like that?
Is this from the conversation I had with Mrs. B?
Could she have called the nursing people?
Changed things up just like that?
What have I done?
I really do need a time machine now,
so I can go back in time and never open
my big mouth.

# WEEK 22

I robbed a bank yesterday
and ran so fast
no one could catch me.
It was because of these kicks, James.
These shoes you got me.
They were like hurricane-force winds,
blowing me through the streets.
And I even let some of the money
driiiiift behind me
like those streams of exhaust
crisscrossing the sky
when airplanes zoom off to faraway places.
I wanted to say thank you to the police for
being sooooo slooooow.
I wanted to say thank you to the people for
cheering as I ran past.
I wanted to say thank you to you, James,
for giving me the world's fastest shoes.
Good thing you can't go to juvie for a dream, right?

*

*You know I'm twelve, right?*
*Seventh grade?*
*I change trachs in my spare time?*
*Rob banks in my dreams?*
Mom just laughed.
Shook her head.
She rang the doorbell.
*I don't need a babysitter.*
Mom's eyebrows went up.
*Tell that to the judge, T-man.*
*Don't call me T-man.*
José's mom answered the door,
just like always, her smile showing first.
*Hola,* mijo.
Her voice smooth,
like a hand on my cheek.
She pulled me into a hug.
I couldn't pull away, so I gave in.
Melted a little, I guess,
feeling her bigness surround me,
her softness protecting me

like those heavy pillows Mrs. B uses,
keeping me still
keeping me calm.
*Thank you, Carmen.*
Mom's voice sounded smiley but tight.
*Levi's clinic appointments can go really long,*
*three doctors,*
*physical therapy,*
*occupational therapy,*
*speech therapy . . .*
José's mom held up her hand.
*I'll drop him at school and pick him up after.*
*No te preocupes.*
Mom's hand reached out,
squeezed José's mom's hand.
*You're a lifesaver, Carmen.*
I can tell by Mom's voice, though,
she's going to be *preocupes*
by a lot of things.

❋

Levi doesn't understand.
He squirms.
He fusses.

Marisol is holding him to her chest.

Squeezing him.

Smelling his baby hair.

A tear falls down her cheek.

I look away.

This is all my fault.

Something that seemed so good.

Has turned out terrible.

Yet again.

*Keep me updated.*

Mom nods.

She has on her I Am Brave and Will Not Cry face.

*I'll be back to visit.*

Mom nods again.

*Timothy.*

Marisol puts Levi down.

She turns to me.

Does she hate me?

Does she know this is my fault?

Marisol signs *brother.*

She sniffs. She smiles.

*Keep teaching him, OK?*

I sign *OK*

because now it's my throat that's too tight to talk.

✳

Feelings, feelings, feelings.
How is it that
I can have so many feelings
that they all swirl together
until I feel so much all at one time
that it's almost like I feel
nothing at all?
I'm not making sense.
Sorry.

✳

Can I still use your computer?
Mrs. B?
Please?

✳

Tiny curls all over her head.
Gray. Like dishwater.
Her face
like someone with giant fingers
pinched her mouth, nose, eyes
into a point.

Her scrubs
covered in clowns.
Clowns.
Really.
Yes.
Clowns.
And her voice?
Fake, high-pitched.
She talks to Levi like he's a dog.
An especially stupid dog.
*Mary.*
That's her name.
So close to *Marisol*, but so different.
I hate her so much
my hands shake.
What have I done?

# WEEK 23

All I'm saying is
you haven't met her
have you, James?
No.
So you can say *hate* is a strong word
and I will hear your words
like Mrs. B says.
I will digest your words
like a chicken log
bouncing in my stomach.
I will let your words
move through my blood vessels
infiltrate my brain
leave deposits of word vitamins
through my whole self.
But I won't stop saying *hate*
because I do hate her.
Also, I do not think Mrs. B agrees with you.
She *likes* feeling words, James.
They are her sunshine.
So don't tell me all these things you know.
You don't know anything.

✹

Dear James,

Mrs. B is making me write this.

You are right and I am wrong.

Mrs. B does, in fact, hate the word *hate*.

Well, I guess she dislikes the word *hate*.

Very much.

Feeling words can be strong.

They can have muscles

and meat on their bones.

They can express your spinning guts,

they can shout your insides to the outside

(but different than throwing up

which you can call *shouting groceries*

if you want

because I read it somewhere

so that's a thing I am not making up).

But feeling words should also be *meaningful*.

That's what Mrs. B says.

Hate is not *meaningful*.

Hate is not *productive*.

Hate shouts groceries all over *more complex emotions*.

You know, writing this letter is making me want to
shout groceries.

Mary makes me want to
shout groceries.
A lot of times, James, YOU make me want to
shout groceries.
And Mrs. B.
Oh, you are the queen.
The queen of spinning my guts.
So I'm sorry, James,
for saying you don't know anything.
Because you know everything.
JAMES KNOWS ALL OF THE THINGS,
JAMES IS THE KING OF EVERYTHING.
Mrs. B is reading over my shoulder.
Her cheeks are so red.
Hahaha.
She is really ma—

✺

Levi was wearing cloth trach ties
instead of the chains.
Thick, damp ties
smelling of sour milk,
baby cheese.

*What are these?*
My voice was loud.
Mary just looked at me
with cow eyes.
*Where did the chains go?*
More cow eyes.
Then, her high-pitched voice:
*The chains are against regulation.*
My loud voice just kept coming:
*The chains keep him happy.*
*The chains keep him dry.*
*The chains prevent infections on his neck.*
My face is hot, my breathing hard.
Mom comes in, takes my hand,
pulls me away
and while I stand in the kitchen
hating Mary
(Yes, James. Yes, Mrs. B. *Hating* her.)
I hear Mom say,
*He's just a boy, yes,*
*but he loves his brother very much.*
Are we back to Levi being a screaming burrito
so many many many times a day?

Erasing Marisol's smart idea of the chains?
That's when I thought about punching the wall
right there in the kitchen.
Pow.
But I didn't.
I just walked out.

✳

I walked out
and went to the only place I *can* go,
even though technically
I should have told Mom
where I was going,
and even though technically
I should have told José's mom
that I was coming.
But here I am.
I won't stay long.
I just need to catch my breath.

\*

Only ten minutes
ticktock ticktock
until Sofia needed to start writing her paper,
until I needed to go back home.
Isa leaned over my shoulder,
her hair as the curtain next to my face
instead of Mrs. B's curtain.
The Google box was blank.
I couldn't type.
My brain was a black hole
pulling every particle of Isa
into it
and forgetting everything else.

\*

*Look.*
Isa stood behind me, her arm reaching over my
shoulder.
She pointed to the screen
but I looked at her arm,
at the freckle just above the inside of her elbow.

It's a really nice freckle.

Round

but slightly gross.

There's a hair in the middle.

A really long hair.

*You're not looking.*

My eyes traced her arm to get to the screen.

Isa tapped the monitor.

*It's not a touch screen*, I said.

*I know, dummy.*

She smacked the back of my head with her other hand.

*LOOK.*

I looked.

*Dr. Samuel Sawyer*

*Cincinnati Children's Hospital*

*specialty: airway*

*Accepting new patients*

We did it!

We found someone!

But wait.

Cincinnati?

Uuugh.

Might as well be Antarctica.

And of course he's the only doctor
in the whole freaking country
who does this surgery.

I dropped my head on the desk.
A hand patted my shoulder.
I peeked open my eyes
saw the freckle one more time,
so pretty
so gross.
Nothing is perfect, is it?

✻

*Reckless* is the word Mom used.
*How would I know you were going to José's house?!*
she asked, slamming her hand on the table.
*How would I know you wouldn't be*
*wandering the streets*
*getting into trouble*
*getting picked up again*
*getting sent to juvie for real?!*
*How do we know anything?*
That's what I said.

Maybe I should have said

But I found him!

I found the doctor who can save Levi!

But I didn't.

I didn't say anything else.

I just stared at the table

while my mind went crazy

saying Cincinnati

Cincinnati

Cincinnati

over and over and over again

*Timothy!*

Mom grabbed my arm.

*Are you even listening to me?*

*You have to be responsible now.*

*You can't go back to juvie.*

*You just can't.*

And she started to cry.

# WEEK 24

I can't tell Mom about Cincinnati.
Not until everything is perfect.
This won't be one of those things,
the things that Timothy screws up.
This won't be one of those things,
the things that Timothy thinks are helpful
until they aren't.
This will be *the* thing.
The thing that makes up for everything.

❋

No, Mrs. B.
I do not think my hopes are too high.
I will make this happen.
No matter what.

❋

Yes, James.
I realize that making something happen
no matter what
is what got me into this mess
in the first place.

✻

For real, though.
You guys.
You have to read these stories.
See these pictures.
Little dudes just like Levi,
who couldn't breathe
who couldn't eat right
who are now all grown up
playing baseball
eating tacos
laughing
talking
all because they wouldn't take no for an answer.
All because when they heard *let's wait and see*
they said, *I don't think so, nerds*.
All because of Dr. Sawyer
and the surgery he invented.

✻

This really could fix everything.
Cincinnati.
Like Ponce de León looking for the Fountain of Youth.
Like those bible guys looking for the Holy Grail.

Like Lewis and Clark looking for the Pacific.
We need money
supplies
a travel plan
appointments.
I am Levi's Sacagawea
sitting in the front of the canoe
watching out for monsters
and following a map
that is in my head
and my head only.

✸

Har har.
No, I don't want a headdress, James.
It was just a metaphor.
Ha! That's a haiku!

# WEEK 25

How many balloon animals equal one plane ticket?
How many bags of popcorn
equal food and hotel and a car?
How many pitches at the dunking booth equal
one fixed trachea?
The crumpled Carnival of Giving flyer.
It's smoothed out on my desk.
We have to get Levi to Cincinnati.
We have to.

✻

Tortilla, warm
wrapped around a sausage.
Coke, cold
sweating in my hand.
Nose, burning
on fire from the sun.
Throat, scratchy
screaming, yelling, cheering.
That's what I think of, Mrs. B
when you say to close my eyes,
imagine my favorite place
my safe place.

Darryll K. Royal–Texas Memorial Stadium
September
Football
Hand, firm
shoulder being squeezed.
Heart, pumping
arms raised in victory.
Smile, stretching
Dad looking so happy.
Just like that
my safe place is ruined
because he couldn't have been happy.
It was just a trick.
I open my eyes and *poof*, he's gone.
Another trick.
That's why I hate this, Mrs. B.
My happy place stinks.

✱

~~Dear Sir:~~
~~To Whom It May Concern,~~
~~Hey, you!~~
~~Hello there, Dr. Sawyer, Sir,~~
~~Hello.~~
Dear Dr. Sawyer,

I saw on the Internet
that you are a famous doctor
who can fix ~~babies' tracheas~~
tracheas that babies have that are not working right.
My brother Levi's trachea does not work all that great.
It is very tiny.
He has a trach to breathe.
I think you might be able to help him,
but we live in Texas
and you are in Ohio.
Can you still help him?
Please write back soon.
~~Your friend,~~
~~Thanks,~~
~~Bye,~~
~~You better help!~~
Sincerely,
Timothy Davidson

＊

*You guys really have your hands full
with this one.*
Mary says this when she's suctioning him
and he's barfing
because she's suctioning too deep

144

and now she'll have to change the ties
(that should be chains)
for the 87,000th time today
and I will help
because I am a nice person
and because Mom isn't home from work yet
and because I don't want Levi to get a rash.
But seriously.
*This one?*
She calls him *this one*?
*His name is Levi, by the way.*
That's what I say when we're finished.
*This one right here. This baby.*
*His name is Levi.*
*You should call him that sometime.*
I go upstairs after that.
Otherwise Mary will call the agency,
tell them Mom isn't here,
and that will get us in trouble.
And even though Mary stinks like a triple fart
we still need her.
*A nurse every day is a luxury,*
or so Mom keeps saying.
It feels more like a curse to me.

✱

The one good thing about hating Mary,
I mean disliking Mary times a million,
is that I get to go to José's house a lot more.
(Only with Mom's permission,
and only when José's mom is there,
and only because the judge said it was OK,
so don't get all sweaty about it, James.)
*Go cool off*, Mom says.
So I go cool off.
By playing Halo
and killing aliens.
By seeing Isa doing her homework
and feeling my face turn red.
By eating as many snacks as I can stand
and feeling my belly burst.
Maybe I should send Mom over there one day,
where everyone is yelling and laughing,
and pushing and knocking into stuff.
Where everything is so messy
but so easy,
where she can cool off, too.
A vacation for an hour
in José's crazy living room.

✳

*Wow, you guys did all this?*
I don't mean to sound surprised
but I kind of am.
The turtle has an engine
where the hole used to be.
It has headlights
in its formerly empty eye sockets.
No seats yet
but there are new tires,
and those tires have zero holes.
*Yeah, we did all this,*
José rolls his eyes, hits my shoulder.
*I did all this,*
José's dad rolls his eyes, punches José in the shoulder.
*With help!* José laughs.
*With help,* his dad says.
*It looks great,* I say.
*Less like a turtle every day.*
They both hit me on the shoulder
and we all laugh.

# WEEK 26

Breathless.
I hate to use that word.
You know.
But this is how I actually felt
driving to Mrs. B's office.
Mom said,
*You're acting really weird.*
I said,
*No, I'm not!*
But my knee was bouncing
my fingers tapping
my eyes watching the
slow slow slow
speedometer.
Then we were there.
I sprinted up the stairs
accidentally banging the door to the office
when I threw it open.
Mrs. B's eyes grew and grew
along with her smile
when I said,
*Hey, Mrs. B!*
I saw the tiny shrug
she shared with Mom,

then we were in her office.
I was bouncing on her couch:
*So? What did he say?*
Just by her face I knew to stop bouncing.
She tucked her hair behind her ears,
she sucked her bottom lip for 1.2 seconds.
*No response yet,*
she said.
I was breathless again
but this time the opposite way,
the punched-in-the-stomach way.
*But!* She held up her hand.
*It's only been a week.*
*He's very busy.*
*Take a deep breath, Timothy.*
*Give him time.*
Time is not an easy thing, Mrs. B,
when Levi could use so much help
right this very second and the next second
and the one after that.
I thought the whole point
of me sending that e-mail
from your e-mail address
was to get the doctor to e-mail back
FASTER.
I will find the money to give to Dr. Sawyer.

All the money he needs.
But finding the time to wait for him?
You can't have bake sales for that.

*

I already know.
I know.
I know!
Thank you, Mrs. B, for explaining to me how it works.
But I already know.
I read it on the website.
You call.
You make an appointment.
But then what?
It's the *then what* that needs the answers.
It's the *then what* that worries me.
It's the *then what* that's making me e-mail him.
When I tell Mom the Cincinnati plan
I need answers for ALL of the *then whats*
plus probably some extra ones, too.
I need so many answers.

*

José opened the door.
I guess I looked surprised
when I said, *Oh, hi. It's you.*

*Who did you think it would be?*

He laughed.

I swallowed.

Because

um

I thought it would be Isa.

I thought I would tell her that Dr. Sawyer
hadn't responded.

I thought maybe her long eyelashes

would dip down

and her dark eyes would look up

and she would say,

*Oh, man. That stinks, Timothy.*

And I would nod.

And maybe she would pat my arm.

My face flushed

and José narrowed his eyes.

He looked red-hot mad

then he said,

*She's right here.*

*GORDITA!*

he shouted

making *me* red-hot mad

and then there she was

and he was gone.

✳

Simpering.
It's a word I didn't know.
I thought it meant something to do with food.
But that's not it.
Simpering is smiling
when you think you're better than everyone else.
Simpering is looking at your hands,
shrugging,
then smirking and saying words that cut like knives.
*It's amazing how long you have managed,*
simpered Mary.
*He really does have complex medical needs,*
*doesn't he?*
simpered Mary.
*We all need four hands, don't we? Just for one baby!*
simpered Mary.
I can't even simper back, because I'm scared.
I'm scared she's up to something.
I can see it in her eyes.
Those big, stupid cow eyes.

✳

*Who are you to tell us what he needs?*
I screamed it.
So loud.

So loud.

My throat felt like I'd swallowed sandpaper.

She doesn't know him.

She doesn't know anything.

She thinks happy leg means he needs a new diaper.

What does she know?

Zero things.

None of the things.

And she's always talking in that baby voice.

That fake, awful baby voice.

She thinks he should be *moved to a facility*.

She thinks he needs *more care than we can give him*.

I give him ALL my cares!

The only thing I *can* care about is Levi!

And it's the same with Mom.

I know it.

If you could die from caring too much, she would.

A *facility*?

What does that even mean?

A permanent hospital?

A nursing home, like for old people?

Could she take Levi from us?

Could that happen?

I want to scream.

And then puke.

And then scream some more.

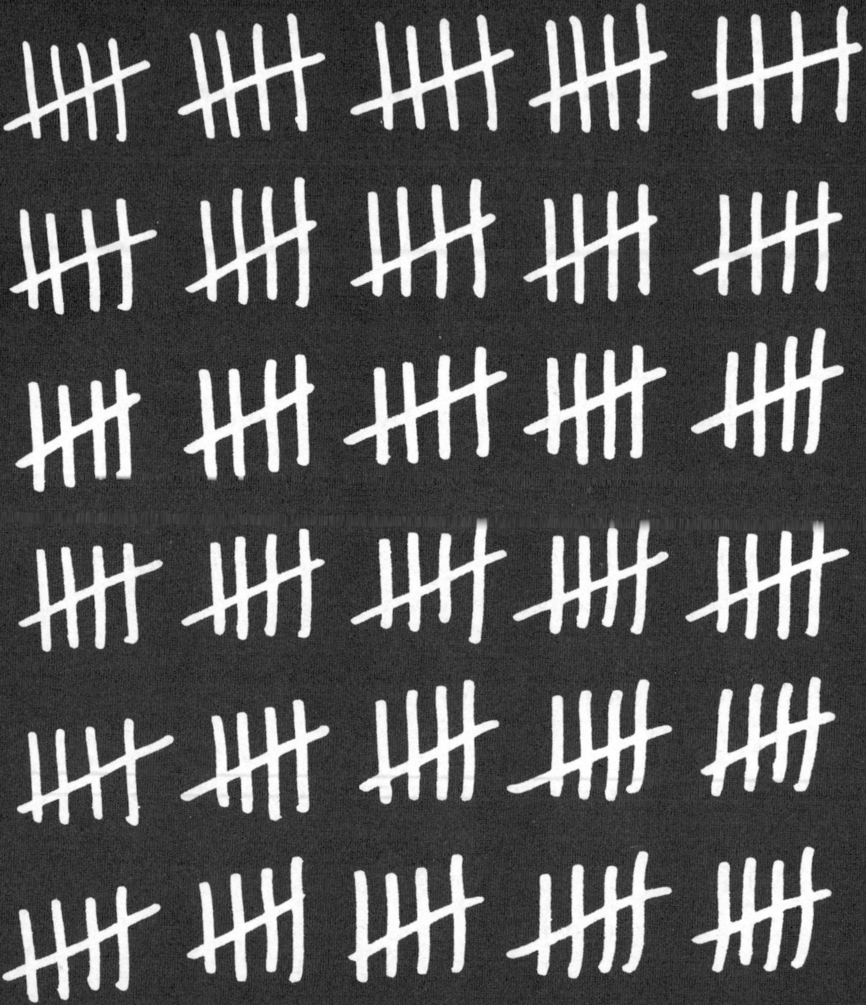

SUMMER

# WEEK 27

Just so you know
I'm not speaking to Mom
possibly ever again.
I can't believe she actually agreed to do this.
I can't believe we're going.
I can't look at her.
I can't talk to her.
This can't be happening.

＊

It smells in here
like the hospital
like juvie
like cleaning tables in detention
like the smell is a warning
ABANDON HOPE ALL YE WHO ENTER HERE.
I hope Mom can smell it, too.
I hope Mary chokes on it.

＊

*A tour of the facility is not a commitment.*
Mom mumbled that sentence
in the car ride home

while Mary suctioned Levi
and I bit the corner of my thumbnail so hard
it bled
red drips of blood.

✳

His head is so fuzzy.
I mean, it hardly counts as hair.
And his eyes are so bright
like there is a power source
inside his head
with extra voltage.
And his smile is so wide
it goes from one side of his face to the other
but not in a creepy way,
not in a Joker way.
And his fingers work so hard
to tell me what he wants
to tell me what he needs.
And his happy leg
goes crazy
just goes bananas
when *Baby Signing Adventure* comes on TV.
And he signs
*more more more.*

And he signs
*yes yes yes.*
And he signs
*please please please.*
So I turn it up
and I pull him into my lap
and we learn new signs together.
And I swear to you
if anyone tries to take him away
I will risk juvie to keep him out of that place,
that *facility.*

*

Mom says:
*The state will pay for the facility*
*if Levi's doctors say he needs it.*
*There's a special program.*
I say:
*Are there special programs*
*so the state can pay for him to stay home?*
Mary says:
*The state already pays for him to stay home.*
*The state pays for me.*

I say:

*The state should ask for its money back.*

Mom says [ignoring me]:

*What if it's just for a few months*

*so I can work lots of overtime?*

*Earn lots of extra money?*

*Save for a night nurse every night?*

Mary says:

*We're thinking about what's best for Levi.*

I say:

*The state will have to pay for me*

*to live in a facility, too,*

*before I let you tell us what's best for Levi.*

Mary sucks in her breath.

Mom drops her eyes.

I don't hit Mary.

But I want to, James.

I want to, Mrs. B.

I want to hit her in those stupid cow eyes.

I really, really want to.

It scares me how much I want to.

✳

Crying crying crying
that's all I could do.
I couldn't even make words
come out of my mouth
and it was so embarrassing
but I didn't know where else to go,
and my journal was stuffed
under my shirt
because it's like a part of me now
and I couldn't stop crying
even when it was Isa
of course
who opened the door,
and even when José's mom
took me to the bathroom
and turned on the shower
and said over and over,
*Mijo, mijo, mijo,*
until she was crying
and I was crying
and she was looking at my knuckles
all bloody and bruised
from punching the wall
instead of Mary

who I would never really punch
because she is old and has stupid cow eyes,
and José's mom was hugging me so tight
I had no breath
and so I thought of Levi
which made me cry even harder
and José and Theresa and Alé and Sofia
and Isa
were all outside the bathroom door
wondering why I was freaking out.
I know they were.
Now I'm out of the shower.
I'm wearing José's pajamas.
I'm in the dark
on the floor
in a sleeping bag
and no one is around
and I can't stop hiccupping.

# WEEK 28

Thanks for the milk shake, James.
I mean, it's not going to change the world or anything.
But it was nice.

＊

Mrs. B.
Her eyes always give her away.
She says she's disappointed.
She asks if I'm disappointed with myself.
She talks about breathing and
staying calm.
She talks about impulse control and counting.
But her eyes dip down,
her eyebrows go up
so I can see right into her brain.
Mrs. B, I might not know a lot of things
but I totally know when a lady
wants to hug me and pat my head.
You were saying things like,
*Punching walls is unacceptable.*
But your eyes,
your eyes,

they said,
*Come here, Timothy,*
*let me hug you and make everything better.*
Thank you for not hugging me, though.

✳

I'm not allowed to talk to Mary.
Not allowed to be anywhere near her.
Mom says it's *forbidden*.
That seems like a really strong word.
I mean, the only things that are *forbidden*
are, like, cursed artifacts
or the entrances to biohazardous facilities
or posting TV spoilers online.
*Forbidden* seems super fancy.
I don't want anything having to do with Mary
to seem fancy.
Mary can be *off-limits*.
She can be *excluded*.
Or maybe *prohibited*.
But *forbidden*?
No way is Mary in the same class
as a cursed artifact.
No way.

❋

I am an island
inside José's crazy house.
Somehow all the chaos makes me calm.
I just let the noise and the movement
rush over me
until I can't hear anything else,
I can't feel anything else,
just José's house.
And I stand still in the middle of it,
a rock taking a beating
from the waves just battering and hitting and
smashing
and loving every minute of it
if rocks can love things
which maybe they can't.

❋

I checked in on the turtle car today
it is still old
and broken
and ugly.
José, though,

had a smile
and a wrench,
a grease smear across his face
in the shape of a
scimitar
like those scimitars
the dudes use
in that game
I forgot the name of,
the one where you vanquish the zombies
with a quick slash
and a yank,
with a plop
there goes the head
or a lop
there goes the arm
or a stab
there go the entrails.
A scimitar on his face
smiling across his cheek
vanquishing that turtle car
while his dad muttered from underneath the car,
*Hand me the wrench.*
*No, not that one,* dios mio, *José.*
*The big one.*

And José just grinned
tossing random tools down to his dad
while I kicked the tires
and listened to that deep grouchy voice
echo off the walls.

*

Mary called in sick.
Hooray!
And Mom had to go to work.
Hooray!
Today is just me and Levi.
I put the music up loud,
held him on my hip,
and we danced around the room
like idiots.
I put him in his wedge,
found a bottle,
and you know what he did?
He signed *music*.
For the very first time.
So you know what I did?

I put down that bottle,
picked up that kid,
put the music on extra loud
and we danced until we were laughing so hard
I thought he was going to have to resuscitate *me*.

✳

Seemed like a weird time for Isa
or medical supply delivery
or James.
Those are the only times anyone knocks.
Tap tap tap.
Bam bam bam.
Rat-a-tat-tat.
On the front door.
Right then I should have known.
I should have known something wasn't right.
Her badge said:
*Carla Ramirez*
*Child Protective Services*
Her face said:
I Am a Lady Who Means Business

Even Though I Am Smiling
Her mouth said:
*Davidson residence?*
*My name is Carla Ramirez.*
*I'm with Child Protective Services.*
*Can you open the door, please?*
That was when Levi barfed
and started choking
so I cracked open the door
tried to smile
tried not to look like my insides were melting
as I turned
ran to Levi
clicked on the jackhammer suction machine
and shouted over the noise,
*DON'T WORRY.*
*THIS HAPPENS ALL THE TIME.*

# WEEK 29

James.
James, I can't even.
I just.
You should have seen her face.
She'd start a question
but
stop
talking
slowly
trailing
off
Levi's alarms were too distracting,
his barfing and choking too volcanic,
the suction machine too loud.
I knocked over the hot water—
you know, from the warm mist?
The thing we put over the trach?
When Levi is on the wedge?
I knocked it on her leg
when I was going for the oxygen tubing
and she went
*OooowooooOooo*

like a siren
and jumped
like a flying squirrel.
She kept yelling over the noise and barfs,
*Is your mom here?*
*Can I speak with your mom?*
And in the middle of it all
Mom walked through the front door
dropping her bag
like she always does
saying,
*Fo shizzle, who's in the hizzle?!*
like she always does
because she is a huge dork.
And this lady,
this *Carla Ramirez*,
oh my god, James,
her face.
I would've laughed
if I wasn't so scared.

✳

*So you finally did it.*
That's what I yelled at Mrs. B.
The words flew from my mouth
like angry bees

buzzing around the room.
She actually took a step back,
the smile leaving her face
just disappearing in one second.
*Timothy?*
*You called social services!*
*You called Carla Ramirez!*
*How could you?!*
*HOW COULD YOU?!*
The bees were in my head after that
buzzing buzzing buzzing
getting tangled up in my thoughts
getting lost in my bloodstream
making my fingers tingle and burn.
I picked up the plant,
the one with crinkled leaves,
the one that sits beside the computer,
and I threw it
hard
against the wall
where the pot shattered
made a loud crashing noise
and Mrs. B jumped back
her mouth turning into a big *O*
and the door flew open.
Mom.

We were a triangle.

No one saying anything,

just breathing.

I could hear so much breathing.

*Well,*

Mrs. B said.

Her voice was a little shaky.

*Well,*

she said it again, not shaky this time.

*I don't know if this makes you feel better but*

*I did not call them.*

*I talked to them when they called me*

*but I did not instigate the visit.*

I let the words settle into my brain

like smoke calming the bees.

*OK*, I said.

*OK?* Mom said.

*OK*. Mrs. B nodded.

Mom went back to the waiting room.

Mrs. B ran her hands through her hair.

She looked at me hard.

A long look into my guts.

I looked back instead of looking away.

I held her stare for once.

I counted like she taught me to.
I breathed like she taught me to.
*OK*, I said again.
*How about a little time on the computer, Timothy?*
Mrs. B stepped over the broken plant
turned on the monitor
looked right into my guts again.
And my guts looked back.
They said, *Sorry*.
They said, *I'm so sorry, Mrs. B.*
*I'm so, so sorry.*

✳

Dear Dr. Sawyer,
You must be pretty busy
with all of the baby fixing you do,
but I am still wondering
how it works
when the baby who needs to be fixed
lives in Texas
and you are in Ohio.
Do we just come find you?
At your hospital?

Make a regular appointment?
And we stay at a hotel?
How much does it all cost?
(I need actual numbers, please.)
How long does the fixing take?
Please write back.
Please write back really soon.
Timothy Davidson

✳

What if Dr. Sawyer finds out?
I mean, about Carla Ramirez,
CPS Flying Squirrel Extraordinaire.
What if he thinks we're too messed up?
What if he thinks *No crazy Texas people for me*?
What if he thinks we could never get enough money?
What if he doesn't care if we DO get enough money?
What if he thinks the *whole family* has failure to thrive?

✳

We're going to need money,

moolah,

cash,

green,

dollars,

Ben Franklins.

If I get it all together

and give it to Mom

she has to say yes to Cincinnati.

Right?

Well, if Dr. Sawyer says yes to the fixing part.

Saying yes to the fixing part is a very tricky part.

So many parts!

Will you be a part, Mrs. B?

James?

When school starts again,

should I talk to the Carnival people?

I could really do it.

I could try to make them part of this, too.

The biggest part, even.

So Levi won't be apart from me and Mom,

and I can be a part of making it all better.

✹

Flip-flops beside my bed
like two dried-up slugs
having suddenly appeared
from nowhere.
I picked them up
put them in the trash can,
the big one
in the kitchen.
I am not wearing those on my feet,
Dad's old flip-flops.
My feet can sweat
in too-small shoes and too-hot socks
all summer long
I don't care
thank you very much.

# WEEK 30

I hate it when you drive the van, James,
the Juvenile Probation van
with that logo on the side.
Do you really have to drive the van?
What happened to your dumb red car?
That dumb red car looks so much better in
the driveway
than the awful van
shouting to the neighbors
HEY JUST IN CASE YOU FORGOT
TIMOTHY IS A SCREWUP.

＊

Dear Mrs. B,
I'm sorry I threw your plant.
I'm sorry it crashed against the wall
making that loud KAPOW sound
that, for just a millisecond,
settled my bones,
a big deep satisfying settling
that said
yes

that is exactly the noise I need to hear
right at this moment,
that KAPOW really hits the spot
so to speak.
I'm sorry if it scared you
or bothered you
or made you think less of me
as a human being.
I will do better.

✹

After all of this,
all of the Carla Ramirez stuff,
Mom can't still be thinking about doing it.
I know she can't be
even with all the paperwork coming in the mail
and the people calling
and Mary saying she'll need a new case
once Levi *goes away*.
I can't believe she's going to do it.
I won't believe she's going to do it.
Levi is the real heart of the family
and Mom is not like Dad,
she could never leave the heart of the family behind.
Never.
Never.

\*

*Don't be naughty, you little brat.*
That's what Mary said.
I totally heard it
under her breath
when Levi was smiling and playing his favorite game:
Drop the Bottle and Make Mary Crazy.
She called him a brat.
Luckily he doesn't know what that is.
But I do.
I sure do.

\*

*She's so mean to him, Mom.*
*Don't exaggerate.*
*Exaggerating would be to say she grows fangs*
*and talons and*
*flies around the room*
*shooting fire*
*from her cow eyes.*
*That's exaggerating.*
*Timothy.*
*She's mean to him. I don't like her.*
*OK. Well. We have no one else.*
*I know.*

*So what do you want me to do?*
*I don't know. Pay closer attention.*
*Timothy.*
*I'm sorry.*
*She's not mean to him.*
*She is.*
*Tell you what.*
*If I see her being mean to him, I'll fire her.*
*On the spot.*
*OK?*
*OK.*

*Good night, T-man.*
*Don't call me T-man.*

# WEEK 31

How would I know?
Am I a plant specialist?
Can I just yell PLANT POWERS ACTIVATE
and know all of the plant things?
James.
Come on.
The one we decided on is almost just right, though.
It is smallish,
the leaves are wrinkly,
and even though they are plain green
instead of purple and green,
at least the flowers are purple.
I am getting the sense that Mrs. B
really likes purple.
Based on her clothes
and her smell.
Is it weird that I think she smells
well
a little purple?
Never mind.

Just . . . thanks for taking me today
to find this replacement plant
that is partially purple
kind of like Mrs. B is
herself.

✺

*That James.*
This is what Mrs. B said.
Not, *Well, thank-you, Timothy*!
Or, *You're so sweet, Timothy*!
*That James.*
And then she got this look on her face
like she was going to happy-cry
which made me feel sweaty.
*That James.*
*He's a keeper, huh?*
And I was like,
*Um, I have no choice?*
*The court says I have to keep him.*
Like James is a watchdog.
A plant-buying,
secret dropper-offer of food,
sometimes red-car-driving,
most times grouchy-faced,

shoe-providing
guard dog.
Mrs. B loved the plant.
And I think she might love you, James
even though you have not met
in actual real life.
She put the plant right next to the computer
and smiled so big
I could count her teeth
even the silver one way, way in back.

\*

I catch myself sometimes
wondering how many wallets
this or that equals.
How many people
not paying attention
could instead be paying
for a lot of other things.

\*

*Oh, hey, Carla Ramirez!*
Those were my exact words
when I opened the door to . . .
Surprise!

Another visit!
From our favorite flying squirrel!
Sigh.
Levi had rolled under the TV stand,
totally twisted up in his tubes and wires,
like a squirming, smiling knot of TV cords.
I dragged him out,
dusted him off,
gave him a quick suction.
Carla Ramirez kept her distance,
not too close to the explosive baby,
not too close to the Joker-smiling big brother.
She found Mom in the kitchen,
washing bottles.
And Mary on the back porch,
having a lunch break
in the sun
with, of course, zero cares in the world.

✳

First Carla Ramirez rule:
*Timothy can never be with Levi unsupervised.*
Second Carla Ramirez rule:
*Timothy can never be home with just Levi and Mary.*
Third Carla Ramirez rule:
*That hot water situation has to be on a higher shelf.*

She said she'd close the investigation,
that obviously Mom is working hard,
and I am working hard,
and Levi is working hard,
and there is no medical neglect.
I saw Mary standing in the doorway
listening in.
I saw her face twist in the shadows
like a supervillain
her look of disapproval,
her head-shakingness over the whole thing.
Fourth Carla Ramirez rule:
*Find a better daytime nurse for Levi.*
(That's not really a Carla Ramirez rule.
But it should be.)

❋

We already knew it was against the rules,
technically,
for me to be at home with Mary and Levi
without Mom.
It's always been against the rules,
but sometimes you have to be bendy
to make things work.
Marisol was good at rule bendiness.
Marisol was good at so many things.

But now Carla Ramirez,
Flying Squirrel Social Worker Superstar,
means business.
So I'm sitting here,
on this hard and dirty concrete
listening to José's dad
grunt and growl and curse
while José looks helplessly
at a spool of something
hanging out of the turtle car's
wide-open trunk mouth.
I wonder what Mary and Levi are doing.

# WEEK 32

When it was late
and you said,
*I'm off the clock. C'mon, let's go,*
at first I thought I was in trouble.
I looked into the deepest parts of myself
to figure what new thing I'd done wrong.
But then we got there.
It was so fun, James!
I've never done that before.
CRACK
CRACK
CRACK
Swinging the bat so hard.
Am I really a natural?
I've never been a natural at anything.
Batting cages.
Who knew?
That was so fun, James.
Did you break house arrest rules
just for me?
Will you get in trouble?
Can we go again?
Yeah?

✳

What do I need?
Good question, Mrs. B.
I need a time machine
so I can go back
and never ever ever EVER
tell you
that we need more nursing hours.
A time machine to bring Marisol back.
A time machine to talk to Dad on that rainy night.
A time machine for so many things.
Can you do that?
Huh?
'Cause *that's* what I need,
Mrs. B.

✳

Dear Dr. Sawyer,
OK. For real. Please write me back.
This is Timothy Davidson again.
Levi is getting sick
all the time
because of his trach
and the germs going
straight into his lungs.

Please help him not need the trach.
Have you seen *Star Wars*?
Please, Dr. Sawyer,
you're our only hope.
Timothy Davidson

❋

This little booger.
He will sign *milk* and *more* and *please*.
He will sign *Mama* and *music*.
He will sign *hot* and *cold*.
He will sign *hurt*.
He will sign *dog* when I need a haircut.
But he will not sign *brother*.
He just won't do it.

❋

I didn't want to say this
but I can't get it out of my mind,
like that red dust in space
that makes big clouds around a supernova
and doesn't move for eons,
that's what this is doing in my brain,
sitting heavy and messy,
getting all over everything else
so that it doesn't matter what I think.

There are little parts of this stuck inside:
Carla Ramirez,
Flying Squirrel Extraordinaire,
she said,
*Looking into a facility might not be a bad idea*
*until you get back on your feet.*
*I can help*
*if you need me to.*
*You just let me know.*
And her card is on our fridge
held up by the magnet we got at the beach
two years ago
when we did things like go to the beach.

✸

Sofia dances through the living room
headphones on
but so loud
I can hear all the songs.
Theresa is out back kicking the soccer ball
up against the house
bang bang bang bang.
Alé's tuba is nonstop
even during the summer
because marching band tryouts
are in a few months.

190

José is killing things on the Xbox
bullets ricochet off rocks and Kevlar.
I'm not interested in killing anything
not today.
I worry about Levi
home alone with Mary
without me there to hear the things,
those things that come out of her mouth.
The garage is the only quiet place,
the only place where my mind can hear itself.
But there's already someone in the turtle car.
Isa curled up in the passenger seat.
Her glasses on the tip of her nose.
A book in her hands.
I slide in next to her,
shut the door quietly,
put my hands on the steering wheel
then my forehead on it, too.
Isa's hand,
light as a butterfly,
lands on the back of my neck.
And neither of us says one word.

# WEEK 33

No I will not ask her.

What is this?

Are you also twelve?

YOU ask her.

James, you are going to make me go to juvie

so fast my head will spin

because I am going to flick you in your beard

if you keep asking me about Mrs. B.

Fine

I will look and report back.

You know she reads this, though, right?

This is not very sneaky of you.

❋

It was like 147 degrees this afternoon.

I'm not exaggerating.

My jeans were stuck to me

in places you don't want to think about.

*Where are your shorts, Timothy?*

Mrs. B was wearing a floaty dress.

*It's so hot. You'll get heatstroke wearing jeans.*

I didn't say anything.

*Go in there.*

She pointed to her tiny bathroom.

*Hand me your jeans.*

My swamp-ass jeans?

That haven't been washed in weeks?

Ha! No way, you crazy lady!

That's not what I said, though.

I just shook my head.

A broken record head shaker.

Then she snapped at me!

A hurry-up, Mom-person kind of finger snap.

So I went into the bathroom, hid behind the door,

threw my swamp-ass jeans at her.

Waited, hidden, in my underpants.

Face hot.

Butt cooling off.

After a few minutes,

*knock, knock.*

A hand reached around the corner,

like in a horror movie.

But instead of a hatchet,

this hand was holding shorts.

Cutoff shorts that used to be jeans.

I put them on.

My knees breathed for the first time in weeks.

I stepped out of the bathroom and Mrs. B smiled,

a triumphant benefactor.

*Those were José's jeans*, I said.

She stopped smiling.
I started smiling.
Then I started laughing.
And she started laughing.
And I thought we would never stop.

＊

Dear Dr. Sawyer,
Subglottic stenosis.
That's what Levi has.
I know you know what that means,
it is like taping your nostrils shut
and trying to breathe through a tiny coffee straw
glued to your lips.
That's why he has the trach.
Your website says
you fix things like this
and since you have a website
I imagine—
and I am only guessing here—
you must know how to use a computer.
Also, your super fancy fingers
that can magically fix tracheas

must also be able to—
and I am still just guessing—
type e-mails.
Please write me back.
Timothy

❋

It's so hot that
if the sun had a sun
and that sun had a sun
and you put all of the suns together
in one giant oven
set on
BROIL
then set that oven on fire
that would be about half as hot as it is today.
Just walking to José's house
I sweated about sixteen gallons
which is exactly what Isa said
when she opened the door.
*Did you sweat sixteen gallons
walking over here?*
Her nose turned up.

*Shut UP,* Gordita.
José pushed her out of the way,
pushed a controller in my hand.
*Aliens to kill, bro. Stat.*
I gave Isa a look that hopefully said
sorry for being gross,
sorry your brother is an idiot,
sorry it is the fiery hotness of ten thousand suns today.
She gave me a look that said
take a shower.

✻

*Don't.*
Mom pointed at me before I could say anything.
Papers all over the table,
a calculator,
Carla Ramirez's card,
an open brochure for
the *facility*.
*Don't.*
She couldn't look at me,
couldn't look at Levi in my arms
signing *more dog* instead of *brother,*

pulling my hair.

*DON'T!*

She shouted it this time,

standing up fast,

fluttering the papers,

knocking the chair over,

making Levi cry.

*I didn't say any—*

I tried to talk

but she pointed at me again.

She started to cry,

ran upstairs.

*Mama sad,*

Levi signed.

*Mama sad.*

*Mama sad.*

*Mama sad.*

He just kept signing it

until I put my hand over his hands.

*Yeah, little dude.*

*Mama sad.*

*More dog sad, too.*

✳

That crumpled flyer
from so many weeks ago,
the one for the Carnival of Giving . . .
it's still on my desk.
Making our family a charity
would probably make Mom more sad.
But I've really been thinking about talking to them,
the Carnival people, I mean.
I really might just do it.
Talk to them, I mean.
Maybe.
Maybe.
Hmm.

# WEEK 34

James.

Stop.

You sound like Mrs. B.

Just stop with the *you get more bees with honey*
*than with vinegar.*

WHO WANTS BEES?!

Not me.

I want Dr. Sawyer

to write. me. back.

RIGHT NOW.

I'M RUNNING OUT OF TIME.

(P.S. Speaking of *B*s,

Mrs. B doesn't wear any rings

in answer to your question from last week.

I saw zero of them on her fingers.

But that doesn't mean anything, you know.

Mom still wears two rings

on her "I'm married" finger,

just FYI.)

*

*Sometimes we never know why people
do the things they do.*
Mrs. B said it with that frown-smile.
You know the one.
Grown-ups do it when they're being
SEEEERIOUS.
*Sometimes we never know why people
do the things they do.*
*But we still love those people.*
*Even when we're mad.*
Mrs. B added in the last part just as she ducked her
head
lower and to the side
so her eyes
and my eyes
were even.
And she didn't blink.
And I didn't blink.
And she did the frown-smile again.
And I don't know why, but
I wanted to just cry my eyes out.

✳

Supplies came today.
I watched Mary sort through them all,
her head-shakingness in full force.
*So many things*
*for such a little baby.*
She sighed big and fake
like she was on TV or something.
Levi scooted over to her
tried to grab some tubing.
*No. Not for you.*
Mary snatched it out of his hands
and I said,
*Wait.*
*That tubing is exactly for him.*
*Why can't he check it out?*
Mary didn't answer,
just clicked her tongue against her teeth.
*Timothy,*
she said,
*you're not allowed to be in here.*
Then she looked up
and smiled.

✷

*You push it with your left foot*
*then shift into gear.*
*It's the clutch, dummy.*
Isa was laughing at me,
laughing when I asked why the turtle car
has two brakes.
*Push, shift, gas.*
*Or something like that.*
*I don't know how to drive!*
She put her hand on my hand.
She laughed again.
It's the best sound,
Isa laughing.
Way better than the
WHAT ARE YOU DOING?
that José yelled when he came in the garage.
The engine still isn't working
it's not like the car was ON or anything.
Though I'm kind of worried
he wasn't really mad about the car.

✱

*Him*
*You*
*Can't*
*Don't*
*Stop*
*No*
*NO*
Mom is on the phone.
I may
or may not be
pressing my ear to the door
listening so hard
I can hear my heartbeat
in between her words.
I don't know who it is.
I'm too afraid to ask.

# WEEK 35

I just want you to know
that little sign Levi did?
When he saw you at the door?
The swoopy thing?
With his tiny pinkie?
That looks like a *J*?
It means *juice*
not *James*.
There's no way he would sign
*James*
before he'd sign
*brother.*
No way.

✻

That phone call.
That phone call.
That phone call.
Mrs. B is worried about me.
The lines between her eyebrows are deep.
She crosses her arms over her chest
which wrinkles her shirt
without her noticing.

But I notice.
I feel kind of important
to worry Mrs. B so much
that she doesn't notice wrinkles.

✸

*How are you?*
*OK.*
*Really?*
*Not really.*
*I'm sorry.*
*Don't say that.*
*I'm sorry for being sorry.*
*Don't be a dork.*
*You're a dork.*
Isa and I can have a whole conversation with just
our eyes.
We're like superheroes.
Very quiet superheroes.
With very giant eyes.

✸

If I stole his Xbox,
if I tattooed *Dork* on his forehead,
if I superglued his hands to his butt,

if I renamed him Shorty McDingDong,
if I ate his guinea pig,
none of these things would make José as mad as
me admitting I like Isa.

❋

P.S. I'm not admitting anything.
I'm just thinking
out loud
in this journal
right now
so
shhhh.

❋

Mary, Mary, quite contrary
how does your garden grow?
With squinty eyes
and big loud sighs
and nursing notes all in a row.

# WEEK 36

No, James, I don't want to write nicer things about
Mary.
I don't think the judge will send me to juvie
because I think Mary has dishwater hair
and wants to break up my family.
So there.
I hate her. For real.
Don't make me hate you, too.

✳

I know hate is a strong word, Mrs. B.
I know you hate it.
I'm sort of sorry I said it.
But only sort of.
And only about James.
I would never hate James.
At least not *every* day.

✳

Timothy's Big Fat ~~Hate~~ Dislike List
Mary
Dr. Sawyer, but only if he doesn't write back soon

The way José looks at me when I smile at Isa
Messed-up tracheas
Dad
Not necessarily in that order

✹

Our favorite flying squirrel showed up today,
all smiles and googly eyes,
cooing at Levi,
telling Mom that everything looks great,
the investigation is closed.
I should be happy.
I want to be happy.
But
But
But
There's always a big but when
Carla Ramirez, the flying squirrel, is involved.
*I'm so glad you're seriously giving it some thought,*
she said,
and my head whipped around so fast
my brain jiggled.
*It's a lovely facility.*
*We're lucky to have something like it in town.*
*And with the state benefits*
*for a medically fragile child*

*needing nursing home care, well . . .*
*it would help so much.*
At least Mom's smile was weak.
At least she looked like she might throw up.
At least I didn't punch Mary in the face for smiling.
At least I didn't leap on the flying squirrel's back
*lucha libre* style.
See, Mrs. B?
I'm learning to control my outbursts.
Ten gold stars for Timothy
as we march closer
to the end of the world.

❋

*We could visit any time.*
*We could even stay with him.*
*There are doctors and nurses 24 hours a day.*
I don't even have words.
She can't be serious.
It has to be the tiredness talking,
the no money talking.
It's not Mom talking.
It's not.
It's Mary talking through her.
It's Carla Ramirez, loudmouth flying squirrel,
using Mom's mouth like a puppet.

*Mom.*
*Look at him.*
Levi, hanging on his wedge,
clonking himself in the head
with his bottle
doing his wheezy laugh
signing *more.*
*You can't give him to strangers.*
*You'd kill him.*
*Everything inside him.*
*You'd kill it.*
Levi stopped laughing
barfed
started to choke
set off his oxygen alarms.
Mom grabbed the suction machine
cleared his airway
gave him oxygen puffs
through the trach.
His color went back to normal.
The alarms stopped beeping.
*I'm afraid I'm killing him here.*
She whispered it so softly
I thought maybe I didn't really hear it.
But I did.
*I'm afraid, Timothy.*

*I'm afraid for him anywhere.*
*I'm afraid all the time.*
*Every day.*
*I'm never not afraid, Timothy.*
*I'm never not afraid for him.*
And when she looked at me,
really looked at me,
I saw how scared she was
and it scared me.
It scared me a lot.

# WEEK 37

Weighing things,
what-if-ing things,
figuring things out.
Maybe I should tell Mom about Cincinnati
even without finding the money first.
Maybe she'll stop with all the *facility* stuff
if she knew we could go there.
Maybe she'd be OK with being part of the
Carnival of Giving.
Maybe I don't need to wait for Dr. Sawyer.
Maybe it's time for a Hail Mary pass.

❋

*You can quit, you know. If you hate this so much.*
She whipped her head around.
I almost expected to see fangs bared.
*Why would you think I hate this?*
She set down the tubing she was draining,
stared at me.
I waited for the fangs.
*I see your eye rolls, Mary.*

*Your sighs.*
*Those groans when you change his diaper.*
She put her hands on her hips.
*I don't know what you mean, Timothy.*
Yeah. I'm sure she doesn't.
Now it's my turn to roll my eyes.

✻

Wonder of wonders!
Miracle of miracles!
Mary is home sick today!
I have never been so happy
to help take Levi to his appointments.
All day doctors
and therapists
and blah blah blah.
But it will be just me and Mom and Levi.
All day.
We'll make it fun.
*I'll* make it fun.
Mom won't even think once about
having to take the day off
and not get paid

because she's out of sick days.
She won't even think once about it
because we'll be having so much fun
at what they call Trach Clinic
but what I call
Super Fun No Mary Day.
Woooooooooo.

✸

At least 20 more months equals
at least 14,600 hours equals
at least 876,000 minutes equals
at least 52,560,000 seconds.
If I reach out my hands
to grab those seconds
like a handful of sand
I can't reach a single grain.
I can't imagine what they even look like,
those seconds,
because the seconds we're in right now
move so slow,
like a big cosmic joke.

And so when the doctors say,
*Wait until he's at least three*
*then we'll see how his airway has grown,*
*we'll see about getting that trach out,*
Mom and I can't even imagine
when Levi is three years old
because we can't even imagine dinnertime tonight.
We can't see the grains of sand
because of all the sand already in our eyes.

✹

I bet it's so easy
just so super easy
to take a
*wait-and-see approach*
when you are not the one
or even one of the ones
waiting
and
seeing.
When you are not the one
or even one of the ones

staying up all night
doing the suctioning
cleaning the barf
carrying the oxygen tanks
wiping the tears.
Yeah.
Let's wait and see
if we all go crazy
or if the bank takes the house.
That sounds like a great plan,
Doc.

# WEEK 38

Hail Mary pass intercepted
on the twenty-yard line,
run back for a touchdown.
Mom: 7
Timothy: 0
She already knew about Cincinnati!
She knew about it before I did.
I guess I should have known.
I mean, Mom's no dummy.
*There's just no money to do it.*
*The travel costs alone . . .*
she said.
Then to herself,
super quiet,
*The travel costs alone.*
And her eyes drifted over to the wall,
the picture of the whole family
in the hospital
on the night Levi was born
and did not die.
We are not playing a fair game, you know?
When even Hail Mary passes get you nowhere.
Not a fair game at all.

✳

By the way,
Mom says those are for other people,
the carnivals that raise money
to pay bills and stuff.
*Look at us! We're great!*
Mom sweeps her arms out wide
like we live at Disney World.
And she laughs
with no actual laughter in her voice
just air forcing its way through her teeth
like leaves being blown against a trash can,
an empty rattle,
a terrible sound.

✳

The kitchen table is like a weird, flat tree
only instead of growing leaves
it grows paper.
Stacks and stacks of paper.
Mom will move a stack
but it's replaced by another stack.
On one stack today, I saw
INTAKE
on the top of a page.

Everything was filled out.
You know what INTAKE means?
It means to take someone in.
She's filled out the form for the *facility*.
If I rip off that leaf will it grow back, too?
If I cut down the whole tree
can I just make everything disappear?

✱

José drums on the dash
his fingers tapping a complicated beat.
He's telling me about all the turtle car things.
The clutch
the carburetor
the brake pads
the whatchamajigger that goes in the whosacallit.
I'm happy the turtle car is looking so good.
I'm happy his dad is letting him help more.
I'm happy about all of it.
Except for one thing.
I'd be way happier if
sitting next to me
was Isa
instead of José
and she wasn't talking about anything
at all.

✹

So many boxes by the front door
like building blocks
stacked to make
a very lame fort.
I started unpacking them
counting the supplies
putting them away,
a job that is supposed to be Mary's now.
But Mary said,
*Wait.*
*Stop.*
*What are you doing?*
I said,
*Unpacking.*
*Counting.*
*Putting away.*
She said,
*But we're sending those back.*
I said,
*Why in the world would we do that?*
She made her mouth into a thin frown-smile,
*You know why.*
And it hit me
like all of the boxes had landed on my head.

220

If Levi goes to the *facility*
we won't need monthly supplies.
I unpacked
every
last
box.

✸

Mom left fingerprints on my arms.
I'm looking at them right now.
Purple ovals on each bicep.
One for every hour of sleep she's had
in the past four days.
All I said was
*I won't let you do it,*
and she just flipped out.
*You think this is what I want?*
Her teeth were together so tight
the words were like quiet growls.
*You think ANY of this is part of a plan?*
*Every day is a lava-riddled path, Timothy.*
*Every day I have to choose a step*
*and decide what hurts less—*
*which, of a million terrible choices,*
*is the least terrible.*

*Do you understand that, T-man?*
*Don't call me T-man.*
*I just want to be able to sleep, Timothy.*
She started to cry.
She squeezed my arms so hard.
*I just want only family in the house.*
*I just want to be able to drive you and Levi*
*to the movies*
*like regular people.*
*But mostly, T-man? Mostly I want sleep.*
Her hands popped off my arms.
Her forehead fell onto my shoulder
and she hiccup-cried
and I wondered
is she shrinking?
Or am I growing?

# WEEK 39

I always thought turning thirteen would be awesome.
A real teenager, you know?
Now it just seems stupid.
Everything seems stupid.
What good is it to be a teenager
if no one will listen to anything you say?
Might as well still be a baby.
At least then people think you're cute.

\*

I saw the way James looked at Mrs. B
when he showed up for the "party."
And I'm sorry to use quotes like that
because I know you all tried hard,
but having a birthday party
in your court-appointed psychologist's office
definitely deserves quotes.
Do not even try to lie, James.
I know.
She's kind of pretty.
Like maybe a movie star
trying to win an Oscar

by dressing up like a tired psychologist.
But I kind of think she's way out of your league.
I mean, her clothes are always clean.
That's one thing.
Also, she is a grown-up.
I know you're technically a grown-up, too, James
but only because you're old.
Anyway. Thanks for the "party."
Seeing Mrs. B meet Levi
was pretty awesome
even if she did try to hug me after
and sniffled a little bit into my hair.

❋

*No. No! Stop that! Bad boy!*
I heard Mary's voice all the way upstairs
with my door shut.
I ran to the kitchen
to see what was happening.
Levi in his eating chair
avocado smeared everywhere
because he still doesn't really eat
just plays.

Mary was holding his hands away from his face
her mouth pinched shut.
*What's going on?* I asked.
*This baby will not listen*, she said.
Levi's leg flew up, kicked the tray.
Avocado went everywhere.
Mary made a noise, let go of his hands,
started cleaning the mess.
Levi looked at me
and put his grimy, smeary, green finger
into his trach.
Plugged it right up.
And then he said,
*MA MA MA MA MA MA*,
and looked at me, triumphant.
*Holy what?!*
My hands went to my hair.
*I know!* Mary said from the floor.
*So unsanitary and dangerous.*
*He is a danger to himself.*
*Just like I've been saying all along.*
*MA MA MA MA MA MA*, Levi said again,
his face turning purple as he talked without breathing,

his smile bigger than any smile I've ever seen.
*Stop that!* Mary yelled. *You stop it!*
She stood and yanked his hand from his trach
squeezing his wrist
hard.
*That's a bad boy*, she said,
*a bad, yucky, dangerous brat.*
I grabbed Levi away from her,
pulled him right out of his seat,
held him in a big hug.
*You're talking!* I laughed,
ignoring Mary,
shouting as loud as I could,
*He's talking!*
*He said Mama!*
And that's when I saw Mom in the doorway,
her hand on her mouth,
tears on her cheeks.
*Oh, Levi*, she said.
She looked at Mary, still on the floor, cleaning.
She looked at me.
*Oh, Timothy.*
*MA MA MA MA MA MA*, Levi answered.

Mom was crying, but also laughing.

I think maybe I was, too.

The first time we've ever heard his voice.

The very first time.

But you know the best sound I heard?

Maybe the best sound I've heard in months and months?

Mom's voice, still choked up, still loving on Levi

who was still in my arms,

the three of us standing together,

a triangle,

a family.

*I'll call the agency*, Mom said, nuzzling Levi's ear.
*Mary.*
*You're fired.*

❋

INTAKE
all
ripped
up
little
pieces

paper
snow
in the
trash.
I didn't do it.
But someone did.

\*

*He won't talk to you.*
That's all I heard
through the door
at 9:17 p.m.
after the phone rang
and Mom ran upstairs.

\*

Caller ID.
The number from last night
not our area code.
I pick up the phone
press the call button
my heart shoots into my throat.
This is so crazy.

Three rings, then:

*Hello?*

My heartbeat is behind my eyes now,

in my fingertips, too.

*Annie?*

[pause]

[pause]

*I just wanted to tell him happy birthday.*

I drop the phone.

BAM.

Just like I would

if it were on fire.

卌 卌 卌 卌 卌

卌 卌 卌 卌 卌

卌 卌 卌 卌 卌

卌 卌 卌 卌 卌

卌 卌 卌 卌 卌

卌 卌 卌 卌 卌

卌 卌 卌 卌 卌

卌 卌 卌 卌 卌

FALL

# WEEK 40

Eighth grade.
What else can I say?
It's better than being in juvie?
Maybe?

✳

Mom lost her job.
Just like that.
Snap.
*Downsized.*
That's the word she used.
She emptied her work bag into the trash can,
kicked off her shoes,
sat at the kitchen table,
and smiled at me,
like she had zero cares in the world.
*Did you have a good day?*
She took a sip of water.
I could only blink.
First she fired Mary.
Then she tore up the *facility* intake form.
Now this?
*We might have to eat the kitchen table.*
*But we'll be fine.*

Then she laughed and laughed
and shook her head
and put her bare feet up on the table
on top of all the stacks of papers.
Why did Mom look so *happy*?

✳

I don't want to talk about them, Mrs. B.
The phone calls, I mean.
Can we make those off-limits?
Can we talk about never stealing again?
Or how I feel about Levi's weird trachea?
Or what we're going to do now that Mom has no job?
I will talk about all that stuff.
Just not the phone calls.
Please not the phone calls.

✳

Dear Dr. Sawyer,
In case you're wondering,
I'm not giving up.
Things got crazy for a bit here
but even so
I will not stop e-mailing you.
We're really going to need extra help now,
figuring out the money stuff

and the travel,
but I'm not giving up.
Not if you can help Levi.
And you can, can't you?
The website says you can.
I won't stop believing, Dr. Sawyer.
Just like that horrible song my mom listens to.
Always believing,
Timothy

✳

Tap tap tap on the front door.
I opened it wide,
ready to say good morning to Isa,
ready to see what surprise she might have.
It wasn't Isa.
It was more of a surprise
than anything she could have had.
Marisol.
Grinning wide.
Wearing her teddy bear scrubs,
her hair pulled back in a ponytail.
*Timothy!*
She hugged me with one arm

and ran inside
swooping Levi up
getting tangled in all the cords,
laughing.
Levi's finger in his trach
MA MA MA MA MA.
Mom taking a picture.
Marisol is back.
Was anyone going to tell me?

❋

*Your face, Timothy!*
Mom laughed and laughed.
*You'd think Marisol was a ghost.*
*But . . .*
was all I could say.
My mouth couldn't find the words,
the ones to say
I thought we lost her because of me
I thought she would never come back.
*Who needs full-time nursing*
*when you have no job?*
*Marisol is back to her old schedule*
*while I try to find new work*

*and then we'll figure something out*
*just like we always do, Timothy.*
*Just like we always do.*
I could only nod and smile
while Marisol tickled Levi
and his wheezy gasping laugh
filled the whole room.

✻

*Things keep happening.*
*So many things*
*to us.*
*But none of the things are*
*things we can control,*
*not really . . .*
*Don't you think it's time for*
*things to change?*
*Time for us to try and*
*control some of the things?*
*Time to let people help?*
*Let me ask about the Carnival.*
*Maybe they won't even want to do it.*
*We won't know*
*until we ask.*
That's what I said
to Mom.

For real.

With my actual mouth.

*It can't be a big deal.*

That's all she said.

With her actual mouth.

Her eyes, though,

her eyes said:

*People will think things about us.*

My mouth said:

*It won't be a big deal.*

My eyes said:

People already think things about us.

People already want to help with things.

All we have to do is let them.

Let them help us.

Let them help us change things.

# WEEK 41

Different greens.
Dark from making a gash across tall grass.
Medium from bashing a hedge.
Brown-green from spinning onto a dirt clod.
So many different greens
smeared across the laces
of the football that should not be on this coffee table,
that should be in Mom's trunk
with the rest of Dad's stuff.

✳

I guess it's none of my business
that Mrs. B isn't really a Mrs.
Though maybe someone should have warned me
just in case I might be out with Mom
at the mall
on the ONE day we go out for fun,
the ONE time Marisol comes on a Saturday,
and we are just walking around
just happening to see
two people I know very well
HOLDING HANDS
and
SHARING AN ICE CREAM CONE.

Gross, James.

Gross, Mrs. B.

I mean, Ms. B.

Or Miss B.

Or whatever.

Seriously, you guys.

Gross.

✻

What do I think about fresh starts?

That's a weird question.

First of all, "fresh starts"

sounds like a grocery store

or a really lame handout in Health class.

Second of all, what kind of question is that?

Mom handed me about a hundred brochures,

all for apartments.

*I was already going to have to do it, T-man.*

*Don't call me T-man.*

*It's either sell the house, or let the bank take it.*

The brochures show happy skinny people

with mirrors on the walls of their dining rooms

and bottles of beer by swimming pools.

*I should have done it a long time ago.*

*I was paralyzed or something.*

*I'm sorry, Timothy.*

*I haven't been here.*
*Even when I have been here, I haven't been here.*
*We need a fresh start.*
*This will be our fresh start.*
She pointed to Bottle Creek Apartments.
I thought it said Butt Creek Apartments.
*Seems about right*, I said.
And she hugged me tight.

✹

*I heard you wanted to see me?*
Her face was all wrong.
Pointy and blinking.
Not soft, not like Mrs. B at all.
But I talked to her anyway,
the elusive Guidance Counselor,
in her native territory of
plastic chairs
and posters of terrified kittens
falling out of trees,
with the words *Hang in There*
dangling over their heads
just out of reach.

I asked about the Carnival of Giving
watched as, the more I talked,
the more her mouth opened wider, little by little
like a drawbridge preparing to let in
an army.
*I'll talk to the PTA.*
Then she paused.
She blinked a lot.
*You know, you are very brave, Timothy.*
She said that last part
as I walked to the door
and I didn't have the heart to tell her
she's mistaking bravery
for flat-out
desperation.

＊

If I stare at the wall,
this particular wall
with the spot
that's whiter than the rest,
the hole that Mom filled with newspaper
and covered with goopy white stuff
and smoothed out with the edge of a ruler.

This spot,
if I stare at it,
reminds me of me
a little bit.
Not quite all put together
but sort of.
I mean, at least put together enough
to rub your hand over it
and call it smooth
like Isa is doing right now
to the back of my neck
while she pretends to not
read over my shoulder
and I pretend to not notice
that she's reading over my shoulder.

# WEEK 42

Levi stood up on his own today.
We jumped around and screamed and clapped.
Pretty much like morons.
Happy morons.
He is almost eighteen months old.
That's when most babies are already running.
But Mom says Levi is growing on Levi time.
That's OK even though Levi time is slow.
Can you believe he stood up?
I gave him a prize.
Vanilla yogurt.
His favorite.

✹

I love that they painted it green.
Because of course.
José's dad said,
*Thanks for the inspiration.*
And he laughed
and I patted the top of the turtle car,
the shiny green top
and felt a little bit amazed

they actually did it,
you know?
They actually took that hunk of junk
and made a real car out of it again.

✳

Killing aliens.
Getting killed by aliens.
Side by side.
His shoulder knocking mine.
My shoulder knocking his.
*I guess you like her,*
he said, running behind a bunker.
I shot a missile
into an alien's face.
*You mean Isa?*
I stared at the screen.
José stared at the screen.
*Who else, dummy?*
He darted from the bunker
covering me as I opened fire.
*Sure,*
I said,
*I mean, I guess, yes. I do.*

His shoulder knocked mine.
Another alien went down.
*Don't be gross about it, dude.*
My eyes burned into the screen.
*I'm not being gross about anything.*
I laid down some cover.
He ran into a building.
*She's my sister.*
*I know.*
I ran into the building after him.
He whirled around a corner
and shot me
as if I was an alien.
He shoved my shoulder,
*Don't forget that, OK?*
I shoved him back.
*OK.*
Then we laughed weird laughs
and started over again.

✳

10:42.
She runs upstairs as soon as it rings.
*Selfish.*

I hear her through the locked door.
*No*
*I don't*
*he doesn't*
*he might never*
*unforgivable*
Then the shower turns on
and I walk down the hall,
back to my room,
my heart pounding,
my stomach twisting.

✳

*As some of you might know*
*we have a family at Honeycutt Middle*
*who is in need of a little help.*
*And because we are a family at Honeycutt Middle*
*we're going to do everything we can.*
That was when I slid down in my seat
and tried to shrink into a dot-sized Timothy.
*In just less than six weeks*
*we'll have our annual*
*Carnival of Giving!*
*So get ready, Mustangs,*
*and let's show the world*

246

*how our family*
*helps other families*
*in their time of need.*
I stayed low in my seat
for the rest of class
not wanting to be embarrassed
not willing to admit it's my family
but feeling my pounding heart
feeling my breathing going faster
just thinking about how it might really
really
be happening
and how we might really
really
be able to take Levi to Cincinnati
if we can all survive
the Carnival of Giving
first.

# WEEK 43

Don't think I'm not counting the weeks
until it's been a whole year,
a year of this house arrest.
And as soon as that year is up
BLAMMO.
I'm done with homework.
I'm done with being nice.
I'm back cruising the grocery store,
back stealing fat wallets,
back to ignoring homework . . .
OH WAIT.
Of *course* I'm doing my homework, James.
Why do you even *ask* things like that anymore?
You know me by now.
You know what I do.
*Jeez.*

❋

I don't want to talk about it.
I don't want to talk to him.
And if you keep bringing it up, Mrs. B,
I'm just going to shout
*SO WHAT SO WHAT SO WHAT SO WHAT*
and never stop

like I have that syndrome
that makes people shout things
without being able to help it.
Except I'll be able to help it
and I'll do it anyway.

✳

I'm sorry I said that
about the people with the shouting syndrome.
That's probably not fun,
to yell things when you don't need to.
Kind of the opposite of Levi . . .
*not* being able to shout when he wants to.
I only meant it as an example
but I guess it wasn't all that great of one.
Sorry about that.
I wouldn't want someone using Levi's nonshouting
in a court-ordered journal
just as a way to describe
how they were feeling
to a court-ordered psychologist
with blond hair
and too many plants
and crinkly eyes
and a bad habit of dating the court-ordered
probation officer.

✹

Did I just do it again?
Accidentally write something insulting?
Or maybe it was accidentally
on purpose.
YOU'LL NEVER KNOW, SUCKERS.

✹

*Do you want to say anything?*
That's what the guidance counselor asked me
about the Carnival of Giving.
She said I could give a speech
if I want
and I was like
nooooooooooooooooooooooo
ooooooooooooooooooooooo
ooooooooooooooooooooooo
oooooooooooooooooooooope
but thank you for asking.

✳

*Go on, Levi.*
He stood, bounced a little
fell on his butt
smiled.
*Go on, show Timothy.*
He looked at me,
eyes like inky pools.
(Is there such a thing as an inky pool?
You know what I mean. Dark. Shiny.)
*Come on, little dude.*
He lifted his hand up
and I thought
finally
finally!
He's going to sign *brother*!
*You can do it!*
He tucked his tiny thumb
in between his first two fingers
like he was making the letter *T*.
*Look at you!*

It's not brother,
but it's so close.
It's the start of my name
it's . . .
He started to rock his hand back and forth.
He wasn't making a *T* at all.
He was making the sign for . . .
*Potty! See that, T-man? Levi can sign potty now!*
*Now he can tell us when his diaper needs changing!*
Levi clapped.
I patted his head and smiled and sighed.
*Yeah. Awesome, little man.*
And then to Mom:
*Don't call me T-man. Come on.*

# WEEK 44

Eight weeks
that's it
all that's left
eight weeks
then no more James
no more Mrs. B
well, if the judge says I'm good,
if the judge says I've learned my lesson.
Have I learned my lesson, James?
I think I've learned too many,
just way too many to count.

❋

I wish I could do that thing
you know that thing?
The one where people lift up one eyebrow
but not the other?
That's what I would have done
when Mrs. B said,
*Timothy, you have a way with words,*
*you really should think about giving that speech.*
*The people at the Carnival of Giving would love it.*

*Your mom would love it.*
*I would love it.*
*Think about it, Timothy.*
*For me.*
For her.
Who do you think I am, Mrs. B?
James?
[eyebrow lift thing goes here]

❈

A school haiku:
*So what's the deal, then?*
*Your brother, he's a retard?*
That's when I punched him.

❈

Things were going so well.
That's when you know to watch out.
That's when you know Timothy
is going to do something
stupid
stupid
stupid.
But in my defense
you can't just call people retards.
That's offensive to everyone

254

with a brain
and a heart.
And if you're going to be the kind of person
who is offensive to everyone
with a brain
and a heart,
maybe your mouth deserves
a Carnival of Giving
from my fist.

✱

I know I'm lucky.
I know it.
I didn't get regular suspended,
I only got in-school suspended.
I wish I had gotten a medal, though.
I wish I had gotten a parade.
I wish it was OK
to punch a kid
for being an idiot
but I guess vigilante justice
is not a real thing
in middle school
or anywhere
really.

✳

*I don't want to hear it.*
*You made your decision.*
That's the only thing I heard this time
through the closed door
after the phone rang
and Mom tried to hide
again.

# WEEK 45

It's too late now, James.
I mean, you can yell at me.
You can talk about self-control.
I can wish I had more of it.
But it's too late.
I can't just go back and erase everything.
The judge will see I hit that kid.
The judge will see I hit that wall.
The judge already knows I stole that money.
What else do you want me to do?
What else can I do?
I am who I am.
I'm trying, James.
You know that.
Please don't yell at me.
Please don't be James from Probation Officer University.
Please don't be that guy.

✷

What do you mean
if I could talk to him?
I would never talk to him.
I'm not ever talking to him.

Not ever again.
I mean
unless he was kidnapped by a chupacabra,
or went to secret medical school,
or was on a hero's quest
to find a forest of perfect tracheas . . .
then maybe
maybe
I would say:
*Why didn't you just let us know?*
*Why didn't you even say bye?*
*Don't you love us?*
*Don't you love me?*
*What is wrong with you,*
*that a human could be so selfish?*
*Do you think this isn't hard for Mom?*
*Do you think you helped us by leaving?*
*Do you even have a brain?*
*Do you hate us or something?*

✻

Dear Dr. Sawyer,
Well, thanks for zero help.
It must be nice to be the only doctor
who can do what you do

because then you can be rude
and never answer e-mails
and people still have to figure out
a way to see you
if they want their babies
to get fixed.
So that's what we're doing.
First the Carnival of Giving,
then we're coming.
And I won't kick you in the shins
when I see you
even though I will want to.
Peace out, nerd,
Timothy

✳

It's almost as loud as the suction machine,
the turtle car.
José's dad gunned the engine
like a big show-off
and filled the entire cul-de-sac
with smoke
that smelled like burning tires
or what I imagine burning tires
smell like.

*It purrs like a baby*,
he shouted over the noise
and I laughed
because since when do babies purr?

＊

Despite my *outburst*
the Carnival of Giving is still on
even though the PTA
or some of the PTA
is grumbling about it
according to José
who was listening in on the phone call
his mother got.
Lucky Timothy,
ex-vigilante,
almost-ex-criminal,
didn't ruin everything
this time
I hope.

# WEEK 46

O
M
G
shut
up
James
you
do
not
live
in
Butt
Creek
Apartments
we're
not
going
to
be
neighbors
what
just
what

✳

When I told Mrs. B about
Mom's job interview coming up
her face exploded into a smile.
Like, it went from
Superserious Mrs. B face to
BAM
HUGE SMILING FACE.
It was a little creepy.
I mean,
in a good way.

✳

A speech.
A speech.
A speech.
What am I supposed to say?
Please give us all your money?
Even though I am technically a criminal?
Even though technically we won't pay you back?
That seems like a terrible speech.
Maybe we should just cancel.
Aaaaarrrgh.

We can't cancel.

But I also can't make a speech.

Maybe Mom will make the speech.

*

*I can't believe you're moving.*

throws shoe in box

*I mean, why so soon?*

throws other shoe in different box

*It's like one day there was a sign . . .*

throws Dad's football in box

*And then the next it said SOLD.*

throws book in with football

*I like having you close, Timothy.*

throws old homework assignment in box

*It will be weird having you far away.*

throws candy wrapper in box

*I'm going to miss you.*

I put my hand on her hand.

I look at the sixteen million boxes

all with two things in them,

all with stupid things in them.

*Isa.*

My voice is low.

*I have something very important to tell you.*
Her eyes fill up her face.
*Two things,*
*actually.*
She leans in closer.
*One: the Butt Creek apartments are just down the street.*
*Two: you are a terrible packer.*
She smacks me in the head with a shoe.
I try to stuff her in a box.
She's so short
it almost works

✳

*Just sign the papers.*
That's what I hear this time
through the door
after the phone rings.
*We've been over this.*
*Sign the [swearword bleeped] papers, Tim.*
The first time I've heard it.
His name.
My name.
It really is Dad.
He really is out there somewhere.

# WEEK 47

Who knew that moving into
the Butt Creek Apartments
would also be a ticket to
James's Gun Show?
Holy muscles, Batman.
You lifted my whole bed over your head.
Dude.

✹

*Everything's coming up Annie!*
That's what Mom said
when I walked in from school.
She was wearing a suit
she got from some place
that gives suits to ladies
looking for jobs.
I was like,
*What?*
*Everything's what?*
And she grabbed me
smelling not like herself
because of that suit,
looking not like herself
because of the lipstick.

And she kissed my forehead.
*I got the job, T-man.*
*We won't have to eat the kitchen table*
*after all.*
And Marisol laughed from the kitchen
where Levi was busy barfing
on the aforementioned kitchen table.
*Don't call me T-man,*
I said.
And then I hugged her back.
Hard.
Because, dang.
She got that job fast.
Mom is on fire these days.

✳

Speaking of things on fire,
José's dad took us out
for a ride
in the turtle car
just around the block,
which was good
because about halfway
I watched his feet working the
clutch the gas the brake

and then this smoke came shooting through the vents
making him grab the fire extinguisher
from under the seat
leap from the car
that was still rolling a little bit (!!)
and put out a fire
in the engine.
So that was way more fun
than the history project
José and I were supposed to be working on.

＊

*Baby Signing Adventure*
Levi in my lap
fingers moving
brain whirling
mesmerized.
I can't help but wonder
who is Miss Jill
with her long fingers
and big white teeth
and singsong voice?
Who is she in real life?
Why does she do this show?
How did she learn all the signs?

Maybe she has a baby with a trach.
Maybe she has a kid who's deaf.
Maybe they needed a Carnival of Giving
to raise money
and maybe she gave a speech
using only her hands
and everyone loved it
and gave her a zillion dollars
and she started this TV show.
Or maybe she's just an actress.
I hate to think that, though.
I hate to think she's just an actress.

✻

He hasn't called since we moved.
Not once.

✻

Who knew the Butt Creek apartments
had punching bags
a treadmill
a thing with those big round weights?
Who knew James would
gasp

break a rule
and let me in the tiny gym
even though I am under sixteen.
Who knew it would be so great
to punch that bag
really slam it
over and over and over and over
until my arms went limp and wiggly
like giant worms.
The Timothy Gun Show.
Coming soon
to some arms near you.

# WEEK 48

You're coming, right?
Mrs. B?
To the Carnival of Giving?
I mean, you don't have to give money
it just seems like you should be there
and James, too.
We wouldn't even be having this thing
without you guys.
So you better be there.
You better.

✹

Maybe I will write something down.
In case I have to do the speech.
Or, no.
Maybe I won't.
Because I'm not going to get onstage.
No way.
Nope.

✳

Clowns.
People on stilts.
A fire-eater.
A dunking booth.
Tacos!
And Levi.
Out in public for the first time
in a long time.
His face was so funny
watching all those things,
trying to figure out the world
outside of his four walls.
I guess that's what made me take the microphone,
what made me make that speech
(without any notes!)
what made me say those things
about my own four walls
my walls made of James and Mrs. B and Mom
and now José's house, sometimes, too.
I guess that's why I talked about
how strong Levi is
how nothing scares him

how he could be attached to a ten-ton boulder
and he would still learn to drag it behind him.
Still learn to run.
I guess that's why I said those things,
watching his walls open up like that,
and how it all made me think of my own walls
and how they made *me* open up
instead of the other way around.

＊

Up there onstage,
looking out over all the people—
holding the microphone,
seeing so many faces—
it wasn't as scary as I thought.
I think I used more feeling words
at one time
than I have ever used before.
And I wasn't even really thinking about it.
I was just talking.
Just telling people how things are.
The feelings came out on their own.
And not one of those feelings
made me want to punch a wall.

And that was something.
That was really something.

✱

Seriously.
You guys.
Was that fun or what?
I don't even care if they raised a hundred dollars,
or a million dollars,
it was just
so
much
fun.
All day, outside, laughing and talking
like regular people,
just me and Levi and Mom
and Marisol and James and Mrs. B
and Jose's one million sisters
and Isa.
Just hanging out
eating corn dogs
goofing around
watching that crazy fire-eater
watching Levi grin and sign

*more more more*
*hot smile man*
*more more more.*
I wanted more, too.
I wanted it to never stop.

❋

A real gullywasher.
A frog strangler
as Dad would say.
The rain just pounding
so loud
so loud
it makes you smile wide
because how can nature be so crazy?
I almost didn't hear the knock
because of the rain
and the howling wind,
but my spidey senses . . .
they kicked in and
sure enough
right there
in the pouring rain
stood Mrs. B.

She held up a piece of paper
so wet it looked like it was melting.
Her hair was stuck to her face
the rain dripping down her chin
and into that little throat space,
that little neck hollow,
like a tiny pool.
Her smile was huge
lighting up the doorway
brighter than the lightning.
*Timothy!*
It was a gasp.
The melted paper hit me in the chest.
*I just got it. I couldn't wait. I printed it for you.*
*Read it!*
Mom came around the corner
holding a squirming Levi.
*Maureen? What are you doing out there?*
*Come in! Come in!*
*You'll wash away.*
So she came in.
Mrs. B.
Dripping.
In my house.

Looking so young
all wet and smiley like that.
I took the soaking paper
careful not to let it tear
and read it.
Then I read it again.

✻

He was touring medical schools.
Giving speeches.
Recruiting other doctors
to learn how to do what he does.
He is sorry for not responding sooner.
He says there is a charitable care program,
a fund, at the hospital
to pay for sick babies who need his help.
He says he has given our contact information
to the people who run that fund,
to the people who give out the money.
He says Levi will have to pass tests.
Not like school tests,
medical tests.
His lungs have to be healthy.
His stomach has to be healthy.

His whole body has to be healthy
so that he can manage the surgery.
It's a tough surgery.
He says that if Levi is as tenacious as I am,
if Levi is as spirited as I am,
if Levi has half of my determination,
half of my guts,
he has a fine chance of passing all the medical tests,
of becoming a candidate for surgery,
of getting his trachea fixed.
He says, *I look forward to meeting Levi.*
*I look forward to meeting you, sun.*
And I can't believe he spelled *son* wrong
but I kind of love that he did.
I really kind of love it.

# WEEK 49

Just a few more weeks.
Then you don't have to see me every week, James.
Well, you'll see me
because I live in 742
and you live in 534
just over there
but you know what I mean.
This all will be over.
You'll just be another beardy dude.
I'll just be another kid.
Don't look at me like that, James.
It makes me think you want to hug—
Dude.
You're getting to be just as bad as Mrs. B.
And that's saying something.

＊

fifteen
thousand
two
hundred
forty
eight
dollars

and
seventy
two
cents
holy
crap
holy
crap
holy
crap
Mom is holding the check.
The PTA lady is at the door.
*Look at this! Look at what you've done, Timothy!*
Mom says it with a huge smile
with tears in her eyes
and she means it in a good way this time.
Look at what I've done.
Look at what I've done!!!

✳

I think about that crumpled flyer
a rolled-up ball on my desk for so many months.
How I thought the Carnival of Giving
was so, so stupid and then crazy and then impossible
and now I want to frame that crumpled thing
and put it on the wall

and dedicate it to the dwarves in my head
the ones that wouldn't give up
the ones named
Scared and Determined
Angry and Stubborn.
Thank you, dwarves,
for not screwing this up.

✷

Levi has a cough now.
Sigh.
That means trach bullets everywhere—
shooting balls of snot
out of that tube in his neck.
It's kind of a superpower, if you think about it.
Once someone gets hit with a trach bullet
they're so grossed out,
they are stunned.
Frozen in place.
If Levi wasn't trying so hard to breathe
I bet he would laugh.
You should see Marisol's hair.

✳

Enchiladas.
Just like the bad old days,
except man, they taste so good
I don't care what they remind me of.
José's mom is in our kitchen
clicking her tongue
talking to herself in Spanish
not happy with our selection of spices.
She is here with José and Isa.
Marisol with Levi in the living room.
Levi sick again.
Levi coughing.
Levi setting off alarms.
The suction machine BUZZZZZZZZZING.
It's strange to me
seeing them here,
José and Isa,
even though their house
is only a block away,
even though it only takes two minutes
to walk here.

It's still strange,
their faces in our new world.
I like it, though.
I'm glad they're here.
When Mom gets home she'll be glad, too.

✻

Stupid germs.
I took Dad's old sweatshirt
and made it like a blanket
to tuck behind Levi's head
so maybe he can breathe easier.
I can't tell if it's working.
Mom is on the phone with the doctor,
the pulse ox is beep-beep-beeping.
It's a little bit crazy right now.

✻

The night stretches ahead of us.
I have the oxygen ready.
If he needs it.
I have the breathing medicine ready.
If he needs it.
I have an extra trach ready.
If he needs it.

Mom is on her way home
from the new job,
from her long day of training.
She is bringing us coffees.
*A treat*, she said.
*We'll watch movies*, she said.
*It'll be fine*, she said.
*He'll be fine*, she said.
I have the doctor's number.
If we need it.

# WEEK 50

I stayed home from school today.
I'm telling you now,
don't freak out.
Mom had to work.
No sick days during
the first thirty days of work.
Marisol had to stay home
to use one of her sick days.
I'm a kid, so pretty much
I can kind of have all the sick days I need.
And Levi, well,
for Levi pretty much every day is a sick day.
Someone had to stay with him
so it was me.

❋

*I'll be gone just a couple of hours.*
*Just while he's napping.*
*I'll get my work computer and bring it home.*
*They said I could work from home*
*the whole rest of the week.*

*It will be fine.*
*I'll be back before you know it.*
Famous last words, Mom.

Famous last words.

✳

You know when you print pictures
and they come matte or shiny?
Shiny is . . . shiny.
But matte is a little more dull, the colors kind of muted.
Levi is matte today.
His face is darker, blurrier.
I wish Mom wasn't at work.
He's scaring me.

✳

Four stoplights.
Why is it taking this long?
It shouldn't take this long.
Where is the ambulance?
Where where where where where
where where where where where

\*

oh my god
levi
wake up
levi
wake up
levi
wake up

\*

Please forgive me.
It's the only thing I can think to do.

# WEEK 51

I didn't care about the cars,
I didn't even think about them.
Have you ever seen a blue baby?
If you have then you know
you can't see anything else
only that awful color
spreading through his face
settling in his lips.
I was holding him so close.
Running,
just running
down the sidewalk
hoping to meet the ambulance
but it still wasn't there
and suddenly José's house was there
and the turtle car was there
and I know the keys are always under the visor
and so I took it
even though it was probably going to catch on fire
even though I've never driven one inch in my life
I took it.
I stole it.
I stole that turtle car.

＊

Did you say five, James?
I hit five cars?
Well, I *was* really distracted.

＊

Five counts of leaving the scene of an accident.
Five counts of vehicular negligence.
One count of driving without a license.
One count of driving underage.
One count of grand theft auto.
One probation: violated.
I'm reading the charges
while I wait for the judge.
These khaki scrubs scratching me,
these white slippers not fitting right.
They left one thing off this sheet:
one count of saving Levi's life.
Which counts for everything
don't you think?

＊

*Your mom will be here as soon as she can, Timothy,*
*as soon as Levi is stable.*

Her fingers gripped the metal table
right where someone had etched
F F F F F F
across the surface.
The surface of Mrs. B's face
was also etched
with lines that meant
timothy timothy timothy timothy timothy.
*OK,*
I said.
*Thanks for coming.*
*Oh, Timothy,*
she said.
*Oh, my sweet Timothy.*

✽

I probably don't need to worry about this journal
anymore
do I?
Now that I'm in new trouble?
Now that I've been taken to juvie
so fast
my head spun.
I like writing in it, though.
I like that Mrs. B made them let me keep it.

So at least one thing from house arrest worked.
This stupid journal
turned out to be not so stupid
after all.

❋

José's dad won't press charges.
He refuses to say I stole the car.
Only that I borrowed it
with his permission
even though I am thirteen.
Is that going to get him in trouble?
I don't want to get him in trouble.

# WEEK 52

Ducks.
Little yellow ducks.
On the mask.
Well, masks.
One over Levi's nose and mouth.
One over his trach.
*Just to be safe*, Mom said.
She held him in her lap
across the table from me.
This one scratched like the other one,
the word *SNART*
in rock band letters.
*It was a blockage*,
she said.
*You did everything right*,
she smiled.
*Well, everything regarding Levi.*
She sighed.
*It only took an overnight procedure*
*to remove the blockage.*
*He's fine now, see?*
Levi smacked his hands on the table.
*The doctors say you saved him, Timothy.*
*Your quick thinking saved his life.*

Levi pulled the ducks off his face
away from his neck.
He smiled at me,
put his dirty finger in his trach,
and said,
*BUH BUH*
*BUH BUH*
and then he signed *more dog*
and my heart almost exploded
right there
in the visiting room
at Tall Pines, Texas Juvenile Correctional Facility.

✹

The thing about juvie is that
it's not like jail.
Not really.
You don't get an end date.
They don't just say:
*You get six months in juvie!*
You have to stay until they think you're fine.
So it could be six months.
It could be a year.
It depends on me.
We're on Timothy time now.

✸

*We fly out next week.*
Mom showed me the paperwork.
*We'll stay for two weeks*
*for tests.*
*Then we'll come home.*
*After we find out the results*
*we'll go back for the surgery*
*if Dr. Sawyer thinks he can do it.*
I looked at the paper.
Everything I'd worked for
typed out neatly
in rows
on a white sheet
just like any old regular paper.
So simple.
So not simple.
Regular words.
But not regular words.
I looked up at Mom.
*You'll have to tell him hi for me, OK?*
*Dr. Sawyer, I mean.*
*You'll have to tell him thank you.*

✳

One year ago.
Like one of those machines
where the ball falls in a bucket
and knocks over a bottle
that lights a match
that pops a balloon
that scares a chicken
who lays an egg
that cracks in a pan
and makes your breakfast for you.
One year ago it all started.
One year ago I made this crazy meal
that I am still eating.

✳

It was weird to see you guys together,
James.
Mrs. B.
In the same room, I mean.
I know you're *together* together,
but seeing you here
across the table,
this one scratched with *BARF*,
was a little disorienting.

And even though it was weird
seeing you together
without any plants
or grouchy looks
I've actually missed you guys.
Can you believe that?

✳

On my cot
in the room
they call a dorm room
though I guess it's probably nothing like
a real dorm room.
The walls are yellow.
Yellow like Mrs. B's hair.
Yellow like the *Baby Signing Adventure* DVD case.
Yellow like the lasers killing José's aliens.
Yellow like James's gym T-shirt.
Yellow like Mom's wallet.
Yellow like Marisol's scrubs.
Yellow like the stars on Isa's fingernails.
*Timothy Davidson?*
One of the guards who is not called a guard
but who is still technically a guard
stood in the doorway.
*Come with me.*

*You have a phone call.*
The phones all line a hallway.
I picked one up.
I said, *Hello.*
There was a crackle, and then,
*T-man?*
I looked at the yellow wall.
I saw the words scratched there,
the words *HOPE* and *FIGHT*
and *BREATHE* and *SUCK.*
I put my hand on the cool cinder blocks
on the strength of those walls.
And I took a deep, deep breath.
*Dad?*

# ACKNOWLEDGMENTS

This is one of those circumstances where the Acknowledgments word count could easily outnumber the actual word count of the book, but I will endeavor to keep it short.

To Ammi-Joan Paquette, Virginia Euwer Wolff, and Tamra Tuller—you brought Timothy and Levi to life. I couldn't have done any of this without you. Thank you. And to everyone at Chronicle—a million high fives for being so darn supportive. I often wonder if I'm the most fortunate author in the whole universe.

To Tracy, Annie, and Chris, thank you for your professional expertise. I am amazed and awed every day by people who work in the juvenile justice system and with Child Protective Services. You are heroes.

To Sam Mirrop, a king among men, a leader among doctors, and the best Tigger impersonator I've ever met, here's to no more Letters of Medical Necessity.

To Anne, Michelle, and Delicia, thank you for your years of loving hard work. When a mother learns she's going to have to share her baby with in-home nurses it's kind of hard to accept, but you all became part of our family. Thank you for being nothing like Mary.

To everyone on our aerodigestive team at Cincinnati Children's Hospital, and especially to the nurses in the Complex Airway ICU and step-down unit—you made a difficult time so much easier. You are amazing, and you saved our lives in more ways than one.

There are not enough thanks in the world for Don and Carole, Rose Marie and Ken, Julie and Chris, Sharon and Adam, all my mamas who circled the wagons when we needed it most, and of course to Amy, who saved me a thousand times just by making me laugh (and making me eat). I love you all more than you can ever know.

Big hugs and loving noogies to Sam and Georgia for having been through so much, but with such empathy and triumph. And to Steven—a fierce and fantastic father.

Immeasurable gratitude goes to Dr. Robin T. Cotton, who, after five years of complex surgical procedures, including completely reconstructing my son's trachea, said to us, "Thank you for letting me help you," when my son was deemed healthy enough to be released from his care.

And to my sweet Isaac—it was a hard road, kid, and you never stopped smiling. You still haven't. I love you, little dude. With all my heart and then some.

# BOOK CLUB DISCUSSION GUIDE

Should Timothy have stolen the credit card to buy medicine for his brother? Why or why not?

Does Timothy have a duty or an obligation to steal in order to afford the medicine? Why or why not?

It is against the law for Timothy to steal. Does that make it morally wrong?

In general, should people do everything they can to obey the law? Why or why not?

Create an imitation poem of Timothy's "confession" on page 7, beginning with "I will never know what I was thinking when . . . " and ending with "It would have." First, count the number of lines in the section. Then, count the number of syllables in each line. Aim to replicate the length of this poem exactly. Afterward, reflect on what you learned about the poetry in the book based on this exercise.

"Mrs. Bainbridge called that last part of the journal/ a breakthrough. . . . I don't feel like I've broken through anything, though./Really./Maybe some things have broken through me?" (page 25) What do you think Mrs. Bainbridge meant when she said

Timothy had a breakthrough? Did something "break through" Timothy? If so, what?

On pages 33–34, Mrs. Bainbridge's questions are actual dialogue, while Timothy's responses are interior monologue. Why do you think Timothy chose this way to represent his reactions? Why do you think the author chose this way to represent the scene?

Discuss the author's use of figurative language on page 47. What is the effect of comparing the mysterious gift to fireworks and a slant of sunshine? How are these metaphors effective in conveying Timothy's feelings here?

Timothy says about José, "He just doesn't even know" (page 60). This is a refrain throughout the book. Discuss who else Timothy accuses of "not knowing." What does he think each of these characters misunderstands about his life? Based on textual evidence, do you think this is a fair assessment?

Compare José's family and house to Timothy's. What do you think Timothy feels about José's family? How does he feel when he's at José's house? What role do José and his family play in Timothy's life?

"Translate" one section of the book into prose. Then read the original passage next to your translation. What is the difference? What impact does the verse structure have on the reading experience?

Given the incidents at the end of the book, do you think Timothy changed, or developed, through the course of the book?

There are many acts of generosity throughout this novel. Which would you say was the most generous gift of all?

**K.A. HOLT** has kept a lot of journals
but none of them court-ordered
(at least not yet).

She is the mother of three,
a lover of breakfast tacos,
and a sucker for poetry
of any kind.

Her most favorite thing in the world,
other than embarrassing her kids,
is to write books
that may or may not
embarrass imaginary kids.

Kari lives in Austin, Texas.
Her journal has a lot of entries
about sweating.

Also by K.A. Holt: